Crazy Tahiti Paradise

Alex W. Du PREL

Crazy Tahiti Paradise

Modern tales of the South Seas

Les Editions de Tahiti
Moorea, French Polynesia, South Pacific

These stories are works of fiction. Names, characters, places, and incidents are either products of the author's imagination or used fictitiously. Any resemblance to actual events, locales, or persons, living or dead, is entirely coincidental.

Cover art by **Philippe DUBOIS**, *artiste peintre* living on the island of Moorea.

4

In memory of Marc Liblin
an extraordinary man and a friend
who chose his exile on Rapa,
one of the last true Polynsesian islands.

Table of contents

MOOREA FOLLIES

THE ISOLATION of the Polynesian islands, the high cost of flying there, and the long years of preparation necessary to sail by yacht across the vast Pacific Ocean keep our islands out of the reach of most people. On the other hand, all these factors also create a rather rigorous selection that limits the number of people who would otherwise decide to recycle their boring lives under Tahiti's swaying palms.

The few Europeans who end up establishing roots in our micro-societies of the atolls or on remote islands are inevitably out-of-the-ordinary individuals endowed with strong personalities. Not to be included among these individuals are the expatriated civil servants with their guaranteed salaries, perks, bonuses and other fringe benefits, those whose stay in the islands is quite short, or the businessmen who open shop in Papeete —a seamy copy of a French provincial town— to try to recreate the kind of structured urban society that will guarantee them a social status and privileges.

The expatriate characters I find interesting mostly live on the outer islands. They usually sneer at Papeete, calling it the nursery for all the evils of civilization they try to escape from. That type of attitude is nothing new: over a hundred years ago already, the painter Paul Gauguin was pestered by the self-serving bureaucracy and the corrupting power of money on our islands.

Whenever I travel to the remote archipelagos, I meet at least one of those interesting characters. I might find such an expatriate on the afterdeck of the inter-island schooner or on some sun-drenched dock where he is waiting to pick up some cargo. One might also find him at the bend of a dirt trail leading into a deep valley or, maybe, as the manager of one of these small hotels hidden away at the end of some deep bay in one of the out-of-the-way islands...

Of course, one must never judge these people according to their financial success. Some, and believe me, they are very few, will succeed in creating some business that will allow them to live in relative financial ease. But the greater majority of these escapists will quickly have to learn the art of survival, of making do, of expecting nothing more of each new day than the strict minimum necessary for subsistence. The weak, the undecided, the hesitant will all quickly give up. Only the strong, the persistent, the dreamers, and the stubborn stay.

The secret of this art of survival resides in the ability to swallow one's pride, to never lose morale, to never fall in the trap of depression, and, most of all, to never, never become bitter. For if you ever allow bitterness into your heart, here or anywhere for that matter, you might as well call it quits... Because human imperfections, rampant in-justice, officials' shady deals, political intrigues and petty bureaucracy all are a thousand times more visible on our small islands and, sooner or later, everything will be known. This doesn't mean that our society is more imper-fect than others, but rather that society here is so much more transparent. So, one has to learn to accept, to get used to it, to choose to see the humorous side of things, and to laugh at all the exposed mediocrity, especially at man's vanity tantrums. This is how one acquires this tolerance that makes Polynesians so special, so social, and renders life in our islands both pleasant and civilized. One quickly learns to forgive, to accept others as they are with their quirks and faults—these faults are actually also our own faults, even if we Westerners are sometimes better at hid-ing them. There is something truly positive in this never-ending lesson in humility and tolerance. The bitter, vindictive, neurotic retired elderly, always moaning about the "good old times" and common in the Western world, are practically unknown in our islands. Our old-timers are cheerful, smiling, and they communicate very well with the younger generations.

But, let's return to our "expats," as they are called in the South Pacific. One of them has fascinated me for quite some time: Francis Melloc. If you ever get lost along the circle island road on the island of Moorea, your chances of meeting him are quite good. A slim and handsome young man may ask you politely for your help to push his old four-wheel drive vehicle to get it started. He'll tell you that his battery went dead the night before. That's when you'll know you have met Francis. Actually, his battery has been dead for many years because he just can't afford to buy a new alternator.

Francis is the creator, owner, and manager of the famous Mana Village on Moorea. This village is well known on our side of the world for being the most advertised Tahiti tourist attraction. You may already have seen its advertising: a gorgeous Technicolor poster showing beautiful *vahines* in magnificent costumes dancing on a large Polynesian double-hulled canoe. "Mana Village and Theater" claims the poster, "Over fifty exotic male and female dancers in a unique Polynesian decor." And it goes on: "Discover the authentic way of life of the ancient Polynesians, their customs, see their craftsmanship live, hear their legends." And finally, "Theater, restaurant, bar, boutique. A Great and Magnificent Show! A Dream comes true!" All of this advertising is of course printed in French, English, and Japanese.

You'll find these posters anywhere, on every hotel's reception counter, in all travel agencies, and on all of Polynesia's airport displays. Most Tahiti tourist brochures include at least one page touting the greatness of Mana Village. Even inter-island flight tickets have the poster printed on their backs, due to Francis' endless drive and his talent for persuasion having succeeded in convincing the airlines' management to sponsor him. But all of this seems tame compared to the dazzling descriptions given by Francis himself when he himself boasts the assets of his village, for he is also a true master of public relations.

Francis has invested his whole life and everything he ever owned in his Mana Village venture, and he wants everybody to share his dream...in exchange for some money, of course, for even the true artist has to eat and pay bills.

Francis has lived the past five years on our islands. His arrival in Tahiti took place with lots of buzz, in true show-biz tradition, travelling all the way to the local newspaper. A little publicity never hurts. So, one day, we simple mortals at the far end of the world were struck with awe while reading the following article in Tahiti's daily newspaper:

« Papeete, January 21

We are happy to announce the arrival in our Territory of the great dancer and choreographer Francis Melloc. Mr. Melloc arrives direct from Paris where he just completed several seasons at the Casino de France. His best-known hit is the show "Go Go Girls for Paris," which he entirely choreographed and co-starred in with the famous Line Peujaut. (See photo.)

Mr. Melloc told us that his trip to Polynesia was a dream he had been hoping to make come true for two years. That was after being seduced by the harmony and grace of Tahitian dances performed by Pierrot Naonao's group "Tahiti Tamure." Indeed, we all remember the triumphant reception that Pierrot and his girls, then our ambassadors to France, received when they gave six performances at the Casino de France.

Mr. Melloc is here to study local dances, which he hopes to blend harmoniously with his modern dance techniques to create a big, high-class show to take on a tour around the world. Mr. Melloc is accompanied by his charming wife, the equally well-known Corinne Dambier, who for more than four years danced with the Pink Bells group at the Paris Alhambra (see photo).

Our Territory is very proud to welcome such high caliber professionals, and we hope their contribution will help to make our culture radiate all over the world...etc....etc.»

After this spectacular introduction to Tahiti, Francis and his wife took a tour of the islands. They were immediately seduced by Moorea's savage beauty. The huge and deep valleys covered with lush vegetation, the lagoon's many shades of blue, and the two large bays reaching into the heart of the island struck them like lightning. Moorea's many remains of ancient Polynesian civilization generate magnetism and a feeling of lost paradise that always captivates any person with an artistic sensitivity.

The shock was such that Francis decided to cut all ties from his old world, give up his career under the Parisian spotlights, and be reborn on the mysterious and fertile grounds of the island of Moorea. Francis fell under a spell. He heard a strange calling telling him to become the new apostle of Tahitian dancing.

This is how Polynesia adopted yet another romantic...

Francis' drive and energy always fascinated me. Well into his thirties, he had the feline, easy flowing silhouette unique to professional dancers. Average in height, he was nevertheless what one would consider a handsome man. His ever-smiling face called for instant friendliness. A rebel lock in his black hair gave him the innocent and fragile look women love so much.

Soon, he settled on Moorea and ventured into all sorts of businesses to try to generate a stable source of income: fashion boutique, instant photo print shop, hamburger stand, tie-dye *pareu* making, etc. Anything was good as long as it could produce enough income for him and his wife to live on the island. But dance remained his passion and so did his dream of putting together an international class show.

A visit to Hawaii gave him the inspiration he had been looking for. There, he discovered the Polynesian Cultural Center village near Honolulu where he enviously observed thousands of tourists pushing to pay good money for the privilege of viewing different South Pacific dances. It was a true revelation for Francis. He finally had found his way, a way of combining passion and commercial venture. He definitely had to create such a village on Moorea, and right away.

Thus, immediately upon his return, he sold all of his small businesses, leased a few acres of land near the lagoon, borrowed a ton of money, and started building a replica of an ancient Tahitian village. Little shacks made of coconut tree trunks, with roofs of coconut fronds and windows made of weaved coconut fronds. Everything was made out of coconut—an entire coconut village in a large coconut grove. It looked impressive. But it also cost him a fortune, as he insisted on great authenticity and ordered the building of many huts. He then hired the most beautiful girls on the island and many handsome young men to bring life to this village.

I'll always remember my first visit to the Mana Village. It was superb. Francis greeted me, dressed as a great Maori Chief in a costume made out of thousands of feathers. He guided me through the village. Here was a workshop where several Polynesians were carving artifacts. There, in another building, some girls were making *tapa* (ancient fabric made from pounded bark). Further on, more girls were dyeing *pareus* (Tahitian sarongs), while, further on, others were weaving baskets. Later, we attended a *tamaara'a* (a huge Polynesian feast) gracefully enhanced by Francis' new dance group—about thirty young people

13

undulating their liquid hips to the sound of the big wooden drums. They made their stage entrance on a huge double canoe while young boys on small Marquesan horses rode along the beach, holding lit torches. Even though I am quite blasé about Tahitian dances, I must admit I was quite impressed. Francis had succeeded in creating an amazing little universe...

But, as is too often the case, an artist's idyllic dream rarely agrees with cruel economic realities. For Francis had overlooked a small detail:

While the Hawaiian Islands are invaded every year by some six millions visitors, the island of Moorea proudly beams with joy when it succeeds in attracting thirty thousand tourists in a year. Thus, if the Polynesian Cultural Center village in Honolulu could manage to attract ten percent of Hawaii's visitors, it would receive fifteen hundred customers a day, more than enough to pay the hundred or so employees of that Polynesian Village. But if Francis managed to attract ten percent of Moorea's tourist "crowd," it meant an average of only eight customers a day—desperately few, not even enough to buy food for his forty employees. Bankruptcy had already been programmed even before Mana Village's grand opening.

After the first few months of euphoria, the size of his staff shrunk like ice melts in the sun. He now had to work with only three girls and one boy and was up to his neck in debt. The only visitor the Mana Village was assured of having was the Tahiti bank debt collector during his weekly Moorea island tour. His wife, the dazzling Corinne Gambier, quickly left him and flew back to France. Their marriage contract had indeed mentioned "for richer or for poorer," but nowhere had it mentioned "penniless." That's why she quickly decided to go hunting for a more productive husband, and before the wrinkles didn't start showing too much.

Despite all these setbacks, Francis' enthusiasm, dynamism, and passion didn't drop one notch. Never in the Tropics had one seen so much courage, so much faith, and such perseverance. Without flinching, he endured all the frustrations of operating a business in a place where the word "efficiency" did not exist in the local language.

Some days, the dance group decided not to come to perform, and Francis had to reimburse the customers he had induced to come with much effort and expense. On other days, the taxi would just forget to pick up the tourists at their hotels, and poor Francis and his cast of performers, all dressed up, would spend the evening waiting.

THEN, one day, Bernard arrived on the island of Moorea. Located about five miles north of the Mana Village stands the Club Pacific, the island's biggest vacation resort. It is part of an international chain of club resorts whose policy is to rotate its entire staff every year from one of its many villages to another somewhere else on the planet. Since the opening of his village, Francis had been continuously trying to convince that resort's management to send him their customers. But all his attempts remained unsuccessful. The Club Pacific had its own activities program and wished to keep its guests captive, have them spend their money in its own shops. So, when the staff changed again, Francis, always optimistic, invited Bernard the new manager to a Polynesian night at the Mana Village. Curious, the latter accepted.

15

With a cheerful character, Bernard, about 40 years old, was a born party animal and an absolute master of activity management. Twenty years of heavy alcohol consumption had left him with a bumpy belly, but Bernard's success and popularity was mostly due to his intelligence and a cunning ability to anticipate his customers' desires.

The night he arrived at the Mana Village, he mingled with the only four tourists who came to attend the "Great Polynesian Night." As a starter, the taxi got stuck on the muddy trail leading to the village. Then, to enter, the taxi driver had to chase the cow that was grazing in front of the village entrance. Francis, dressed up with his impressive feathered costume, greeted them and guided them through the village. After the several past years of operation, the buildings were run down, many of the thatched roofs had holes in them, and the wood-carving shop was leaning about ten degrees, somewhat like the Tower of Pisa, because the termites and rot had eaten away the bases of some of the coconut trunks that supported the roof.

After the small group had watched the woodcarver at work, Francis walked very slowly while explaining what they were about to see next: how to prepare coconut milk. When they entered that hut, it turned out that the coconut grater was the Polynesian who had been the sculptor, but wearing a different *pareu*. In the next hut, the *vahine* dyeing the *pareu* was again the same Tahitian, but this time he was wearing a wig and his *pareu* was wrapped around him woman's style; his long fake hair was hanging in his face so he wouldn't be recognized.

And in every single hut, they kept seeing the same native over and over again. As it turned out, the "authentic Polynesian village" had only one craftsman with an obvious talent for very quick wardrobe changes.

Then came the "Tahitian feast." Now, it was Francis' turn to play all the roles; he was the canoe paddler when the dance group arrived, consisting of three cute Tahitian girls, one of whom would not open her mouth because she had forgotten her denture at home. Francis was the horse rider and then the groom in the Polynesian wedding ceremony. He climbed up a coconut tree in a *pareu* to show how to pick a coconut. Later, he was the Master of Ceremony and the native Chief during the dance show. He quickly returned to be also the waiter and the bartender when dinner was served. Then, finally, he was the cashier, the host, and the cab driver when it was time for the customers to leave.

In his well-traveled life, seldom had Bernard witnessed such a pitiful show staged with so few resources. The village's tacky buildings gave it an Edgar Alan Poe story mood, adding a tragic dimension to the spectacle. He thanked his host and left. After seeing his guest's gloomy face, Francis knew it wasn't this year that he would be entertaining the numerous customers of the Club Pacific tourist treadmill.

Thus, one can imagine his surprise when, three days later, he received a reservation call for thirty Club Pacific guests for the following Wednesday...and twenty-two for Thursday...and twenty-seven for Saturday! He was euphoric. Since he was alone and no one was there to push start the pick-up, he jumped on his bicycle and rushed out to the club to thank Bernard.

"Thank you so much, Bernard. You saved my life! And I thought you didn't enjoy the show...," said Francis, still out of breath.

"Of course I did! You have a worthwhile show in your village. A rather unique show, if I may say so."

"I knew that some day, someone would recognize my talents. Don't my girls dance well? I taught them everything. And you saw my village? Quite a sight, huh? A true living museum."

"Yes, great.... Listen, I'll be sending you customers as often as I can. Come to see me once in a while and tell me how things are going. I only have one condition: my customers must be satisfied. You know that when they leave here, they have to fill out a questionnaire that goes straight to the corporate office in Paris. So, I'm counting on you to pamper them."

Francis pedaled joyfully all the way back. He figured one hundred and sixty customers a week at least; that meant he could start paying back his loans. The bank would extend him credit. He was saved! A true believer always wins!

And Bernard did keep his promise. Customers were swarming every night except Friday, which was "Cabaret Night" at the Club Pacific. Francis chose that day to go to there to thank Bernard, who assured him that all the customers were happy and all saw their visit to the village as a cultural highlight.

After three successful weeks, Francis started feeling better. He even told Bernard that he was hiring a few more waitresses and dancers.

Unfortunately, no guests of Club Pacific showed up the following two weeks. He went back several times to the Club Pacific to talk to Bernard.

"I don't see any of your guests anymore? Did someone complain about something?"

"No, no complaints, but our guests are kind of strange right now. Even the other excursion operators have noticed. Believe me, I'm trying all I can to talk them into going to your village, but they are just not interested. Listen, I can't just stick a gun in their backs to force them to go see your show!"

"That means I'll have to lay off the new people. These past two weeks, I have lost all the money I made the previous three weeks..."

The following Saturday, however, the customers returned. This time business boomed for a whole month. Then, again, nobody came for a while. Francis was going from euphoria to depression over an average five-week cycle. Each time he thought business was finally booming and established, another group of reluctant guests would arrive at the Club Pacific and, despite Bernard's efforts, he would be back at the brink of a financial cliff.

It went on like this all the time. Francis was running like a madman, frantically passing out his brochures and satisfying his bankers with mountains of papers and figures. Luckily, Bernard remained his true friend. The Club Pacific guests kept Francis alive, even if he was still up to his neck in debt.

A WHOLe year had gone by, and, as scheduled, Bernard's stay in Moorea came to an end. A very sad Francis arrived at the going-away party organized by the Tahitian Club Pacific employees for their departing manager. Francis was carrying his present for Bernard, a huge wooden *tiki* (Polynesian god figure) carved out of a coconut log. He was hoping, not too much so, that Bernard's successor would continue to sell to the guests the merits of his Mana Village.

He had already downed two glasses of Scotch when Bernard joined him at the bar.

"Come, let's have a drink on the beach. I've got to talk to you."

Francis grabbed his glass and dragged the large *tiki* to follow Bernard. They sat on of the lounge chairs by the lagoon, under a sky full of stars, away from the crowd. Bernard started to talk.

"I'll be leaving tomorrow. This past year in Moorea has been a magnificent one for me. But before I leave, I wanted to talk to you because I owe you an explanation."

"No, no," interrupted Francis, "I'm the one who must thank you. You saved my village and you are the first person who really appreciates my art. I'll be forever grateful. You must know I consider you my very best friend."

"Wait a minute, cool a little, listen to me first. You see, large resort chains like Club Pacific are going through a lot of adjustments. The world around us is changing fast, and we have to adapt. In the past, our three big sales arguments have always been 'Sun, Sea, and Sex,' with piles of food added. But this isn't selling anymore. People are becoming more and more conscious of the importance of a well-balanced diet and of moderate alcohol consumption. Then, the HIV virus and AIDS turned our cute little sexual circus into a sad Russian roulette. So, what do we have left to offer? Of course, we have sports, diving, and relaxing. But you can find those same things in any other hotels. So, we had to be creative and invent new attractions to remain competitive. Our club now serves light and modern cuisine, and, most important, we have added a new dimension, the cultural dimension."

"And, of course, that's where my village happens to be at the right time and the right place! Where your customers can discover the wonders of ancient Tahitian culture and its glorious dances!" Francis was glowing with pride.

"Not quite, not quite... but you interested me. Listen now! I'll be honest, and you'll understand. The first time you invited me, I was stunned by your guts to put on such a show. Your village is falling apart and collapsing. Your roofs are full of holes. If you keep quiet in one of your huts, you can hear the termites munching away your coconut rafters. Your outrigger canoes are rotten, and they leak. Your horse is limping. Your costume is missing half its feathers. You have almost no staff. Even your girls look sad. Then, for a grand finale, your customers have to push your old car through the mud and chase cows so you can bring them back to their hotel. The whole thing borders on ridiculous, on contemptuous. It's a joke. You must be the only person who has ever created a slum made out of coconut leaves and logs. Sending my customers to such a dive seemed out of the question; I thought that they would have felt cheated."

Francis' face had turned red, and he interrupted Bernard, "That's not true; you're lying! All the customers you sent told me how much they enjoyed my show. Even yourself! You also read to me some of the comments they left on the questionnaires; everybody loved it."

"I know, I know... But will you just let me finish my explanation... That night, when I returned to the club, I thought about your problem. This is when I realized that your village featured something that was really worth a visit. A human factor! And all I had to do was to explain it properly to my clients before sending them to your slum... You see, most of the visitors to Tahiti, at least the ones from the older generations, have read the classic books about Tahiti and the South Pacific: Somerset Maugham, James Michener, Jack London, some even Stevenson, O'Brien, or Melville.

21

Alex W. du PREL

"...And what do you think these stories are about? They are about the troubles and hardships of Western expatriates on exotic tropical islands. They talk about interesting and often unique characters stuck in the existential dead end that an island can sometimes become. Many of our members are eagerly seeking this kind of encounter. For them, being able to witness live human drama on faraway islands is a great cultural experience. So, with each new arrival of guests, I gave the following speech:

'If you are interested in an offbeat human specimen, not far from the Club Pacific we have a perfect example of a Gauguin-style romantic. He is a man desperately fighting on, a master of survival. A former more or less famous Parisian dancer, he created a truly bizarre enterprise. It is called Mana Village, and it should have gone bankrupt, even collapsed a long time ago. But, and this is where the man is truly unique, he will do anything—absolutely anything— so he won't have to admit the failure of his dream. His supply of energy is inexhaustible and his optimism unshakable. If you go to his village, you'll see him run, climb, dance, row, ride his horse, cook, serve, drive. He does everything, so he won't have to admit that his project won't fly. He'll show you a pitiful dance show, and he'll serve you strange food of dubious freshness, so don't eat too much of it. The real show is this man; he is one hundred percent artist, a real Tahiti nut ready to die for his dream, his ideal.'

"My customers adore this kind of story and love to talk about their visit after having seen your show. This is how you have become the Club Pacific's best intellectual conversation piece... our great attraction."

In between, Francis had turned white. He was stuttering,

"But...but...no, that's a joke. You are just being mean...cruel. It's not true.... See, sometimes, nobody would come.... You see, you are lying!"

"No. I'm not lying. Because people stopped coming every time I stopped making my little speech."

Francis, deeply hurt, was shouting now, "Why then? If it is such an intellectual thrill to watch me struggle. Why?"

"Because after three weeks of steady customers, you had a steady income and you were smiling again, you were looking more relaxed, you were even hiring more Tahitians. And the show would start to lose its credibility. Instead of a shoestring Mickey Mouse "cultural village," we had a little business with a smiling boss. And that killed the show! So, *skweek*! I turn the faucet off for two weeks. No more income. Your banker harasses you again, the debt collector returns, the rope tightens again around your neck. You become restless again. You run again like a chicken with its head cut off. The show is authentic again.... I can't afford to disappoint my customers."

Francis, pale, mouth gaping, stared at him with bulgy eyes. He was speechless. Bernard got up and adjusted his *pareu*.

"Come. Let's have a drink at the bar, and then let's have dinner. We've got tons of grilled lobster with some great little Riesling wine.... You'll enjoy it." And Bernard walked away toward the large cocktail lounge where the other invited guests were gathered.

Five minutes later, while drinking some champagne with the island chief and other officials, Bernard heard a loud crashing noise coming from the bar. He excused himself to find out what was happening, but the bartender was already running up him.

"It's Francis! He suddenly went mad! He walked quietly up to the bar; then, all of a sudden, he picked up his huge wooden *tiki* and threw it into the liquor display shelves. Almost all the bottles are smashed; the guests are skating in booze. What shall I do? Call the police?"

"No, that's all right. Make no fuss. Set up a makeshift bar right away, clean up, and forget it."

The following day, Bernard left Moorea on the noon flight. Again, all morning, his departure had been celebrated with mountains of flowers, flowing champagne, songs, dances, hugs and shell leis, all in true Tahitian and Club Pacific tradition, right up to the plane stairway.

At the same time, a few miles away, on the ferry dock, a lonely Francis, flyers in hand, was harassing a dozen lost tourists fresh off the Tahiti boat.

"Mana Village! Mana Theater! The Polynesian Dream! Come and visit..."

The *"Ori"* of the Vahine

POOR Jean-Pierre. He had fallen madly in love. He fell in love with a young Tahitian *vahine*, a superb girl named Vaitiare.

And one must admit that here was something to fall in love with. Vaitiare is really an exceptional girl. An unusual beauty. Tall but not too much, she has the prominent cheekbones of Polynesians, large round dark eyes in which one would like to drown, plus a softness, the timidity of innocence which instills into men the urge to protect such an apparently fragile creature.

And her body! Sublime. The long legs. The posterior muscular and arrogant. Firm and teasing breasts. All this dominated by long and smooth charcoal hair that ripples like the echo of its flexible approach and elegant movements conditioned by several years of learning Tahitian dance. A dream come true, this *vahine*!

So why poor Jean-Pierre?

Because Vaitiare , this cheerful and idyllic creature, is only eighteen years old. In Tahiti, this is not a small detail you cannot afford to forget.

All his colleagues had warned Jean-Pierre, a doctor recently transferred from Metropolitan France:

- "You just can't fall in love with a girl so young. Be reasonable, come on!"

But love is what we know it to be. It turns perfect eyesight into blindness and fear into daring. Dazzled by so much youth and femininity, Jean-Pierre could only be a victim of the sequels of his irrational and boundless passion. He saw only Vaitiare. He thought only Vaitiare. Every whim of this charming exotic creature became an order for him to obey to. Her every change of mood seemed a nightmare for Bernard. Every minute without her seemed endless. Thus he did deliberately tie himself with indestructible chains to the kind of love that only madmen can forge. Poor Jean-Pierre!

Yet there were lots of reasons for him not to fall into such a trap. One reason that he just had gone through a painful and costly divorce to be able to extricate himself from a stupid youth marriage that did not, thank God, produce any children. He even had vowed to remain a bachelor for at least two years, to be able to regain some balance. Fate would have it otherwise. Less than two weeks after his arrival in Tahiti, his path crossed that of the beautiful Vaitiare.

Unfortunately, Jean-Pierre still bore within himself the legacy of many years living next to his domineering and possessive former wife. Thus, a deep insecurity, amplified by the gossip and rumors concerning Tahitian ladies, made him doubt about his ability to keep this exceptional girl. And insecurity means jealousy. And jealousy in a love relationship equals to true hell. Poor Jean-Pierre. Being of the jealous kind and falling in love with a Tahitian goddess eighteen years of age can only result in great pain.

Namely because in Tahiti there is the phenomenon of the *"ori"*.

The *"ori"* (literally dancing, also called *"taurearea"*), is an old and very healthy custom performed by a lot of young girls and boys of our islands. Early in their adulthood, they spend several months or even years enjoying their freedom, making the best of their youth and taste all the pleasures adult life offers before settling in the serious part of life, and that of a lasting union. All this serves as a school to infuse the values of society outside the family and to acquire the necessary experience to be able to satisfy and keep a spouse.

This *"ori"* is actually a very sane custom. It is a much smarter, and above all more honest way to completely unwind before going into marriage. Much less hypocritical than being married in the scent of virginity only to later slip into the sordid deceptions and sick lies linked to any extramarital affair.

Vaitiare, with the freshness of her eighteen years, was just beginning the investigative phase of her life. For her, Jean-Pierre was a very nice encounter, but it was only an encounter. She was much touched by the boundless attention this mature and educated man showed her. Seeing his devotion was very helpful for her to fight and control

the doubts and insecurities felt by a youth whose personality develops.

But the European sense of exclusive property that Jean-
Pierre expressed toward her made her feel increasingly
uncomfortable. Even an innocent conversation with a
former school friend now triggered reprimands. The
pleasure she once felt of going with him to nightclubs of
Papeete had been gradually replaced by the fear of a
scene in front of other people. And this tension made her
infinitely sad.

So, inevitably, one night after yet another scene of jealousy, she disappeared.

Jean Pierre spent two days and two sleepless nights
waiting for her. He was tortured by worry. His entire
world, centered on the young beauty, just fell apart.

Driven by terrible doubts and imagination, he finally
decided to go to the police to report the disappearance of
his girlfriend.

At the police station, an officer listened respectfully to
his explanation, but refused to start a missing person research:

- "Come on, come-on! You, a thirty-five years old man.
You're in love with a girl of eighteen. You are neither
family nor married to her. And she leaves after what appears to be a argument. Well, she must be staying with a
girlfriend or with another man, just to breathe a bit. Be
reasonable! She will come back, or send someone to collect her belongings. Calm down! You must give her time.
Come, come, you're not a child. Show some courage! "

It was exactly what Jean-Pierre had dreaded to hear:
"... or with another man .." He left the police station as
disgraceful, head down, feeling stifled jealousy.

There is no need here to describe the next two weeks of ordeal that jealousy and anxiety made suffer a man issued from a society that has strict rules about the definition of property. He stayed at home, even feigning illness to avoid having to face his colleagues at the hospital.

THEN one morning, as predicted by the police officer, Vaitiare suddenly reappeared, radiant, happy and fresh, wrapped in a blue *pareu*, carrying her basket made of woven pandanus with the handles over one shoulder. She leaned over Jean Pierre, still in bed, and gave him one big noisy kiss on the forehead.

- "How are you, darling? I hope you didn't get too bored?" she asked with her lovely and melodious Tahiti accent.

Jean Pierre gasped a few seconds. He fought two emotions: the joy of having Vaitiare back next to him and the fear of obtaining an explanation for her long, long absence. Overjoyed, he took her in his long arms, then pushed her slowly away, looking at her:

- "Ah, you're well! Too well, perhaps. Where have you been? "

- "Well ..., I just had to change a bit... You know, you make too many scenes; it's just *"fiu roa"* (overdose)! "

- "Where were you? I called your mother ... I called your friends. You were not at home. You were not with them. I know it! So? Where were you? "

- "Calm down, I came back, didn't I? "

Jean-Pierre was now certain she had had an affair with another man. The demon of jealousy seized him and began to speak loudly:

- "You cheated on me. Admit it! I know! Come on, tell me! "

Vaitiare did not answer. Instead she just went to the center of the room and started undressing. The slippers flew to one side of the room. The *pareu* fell on the floor. She then slowly lowered her panties and kicked them away to land next to the slippers. Then she joined her hands behind her neck and slowly raised them, thus pulling her long hair up over her head. Thus, stark naked, she made several slow spins, revealing all the beauty and delights of her superb copper colored body and jet black pubic hair. Jean-Pierre was even more furious now, even though he also felt his manhood rise in him:

- "Stop your circus! Answer me! You cheated on me! Admit it! No need to try to excite me, it will not work!"

Vaitiare continued to spin slowly. Then, facing him again, she softly answered with an enchanting smile:

- "No, darling, I do not want to get you excited. I just want to show you. Look carefully. Examine every detail! As you can see, nothing is missing. Nothing is damaged. I'm still the same... Just look... Everything is there, just as before...

"So, what are you complaining about?"

The Bora Bora Chest

IT WAS one of those tropical mornings that remain forever engraved in your memory; one of those austral winter mornings in Polynesia. The blue of the sky was deep and dense, as if it had been photographed through a polarizing filter. The sun had just risen and was lighting the whole island with its warm, yellow glow. To my right, Bora Bora's lagoon spread out like a mirror, and to the left, the gigantic Otemanu Mountain loomed like an eternal and impregnable fortress. Not a breath of wind wrinkled the surface of the lagoon, and one could see clearly in the water every coral outgrowth, even the deep ones. As the morning had a freshness, which is far too rare in the tropics, I drove my old Citroën buggy slowly so that I could appreciate the rapture of the moment.

I had decided to pay a visit to Tihoni on Matira Point, to see if he had a few lobsters to sell. It had been a moon-less night, and the ocean was calm, disturbed only by a long swell, the remnant of some lost storm way south off the coast of Antarctica. All of these were unerring signs that Tihoni must have gone on the reef to catch some lob-sters; these little beasts that I rank as one of the best meals that man can appreciate, especially when barbe-cued and served with a butter-garlic sauce. So my lust for food (just as my customers') was the reason I syn-chronized my rising with that of the chickens. Indeed, should I show up at my friend the fisherman at a sup-posedly more civilized hour, the cooks from the island's big luxurious hotels would have already grabbed all the bounty from "the man who walks the reef at night with a kerosene lamp."

As my plastic car drove through a coconut grove, I saw a woman making energetic hand signals by the side of the road. I slowed down. It was Madame Dorita, Jacqui's wife. In our islands, people are known only by their first names or nicknames, because in Polynesia, family names are too complicated to memorize, let alone to pronounce.

"Stop over on your way back! I'm preparing coffee!" she called.

I kept on driving. Madame Dorita knew very well where I was going, and understood that being late could mean missing the purpose of my early morning journey. The coffee offer meant that she needed something.

One hour later, six big lobsters, each over three pounds, were kicking their tails in a bucketful of sea water attached to the flatbed at the rear of the Citroën, their long whiskers sticking out and moving in all directions. I parked the automobile in Madame Dorita's yard. She was waiting, sitting at the kitchen table. A steaming cup of coffee and a few slices of buttered bread sat on the plastic tablecloth, readywaiting for me. I gave her a kiss on both cheeks and sat down on the bench opposite her.

"Thanks for coming. It's my washing machine... Yes, I know, it's a luxury item and a *vahine* (Polynesian woman) is supposed to wash by hand... But, as you know, I rent bungalows to tourists, and some days I have to wash at least a dozen sheets... By hand, that's just too much. I heard you even fixed Maco's TV last week..."

I watched her with a smile, while chewing on my bread. There was no need for an answer. Of course, I was going to check her machine. At the time, no mechanic lived on the island. Even so, it was not my job. The rumor had long flown around the island that the boss of the Yacht Club was gifted for things mechanical. It didn't bother me at all. Helping each other was just a part of island life. Making someone happy is still one of the great pleasures left in this evil world. And above all, it allowed me to get to know a kind and spontaneous people rather well.

Only once did I regret my brotherly gestures: the French principal at the island's small high school once asked me to repair his photocopy machine (only a gear was unscrewed). But from that day on, I was nothing more than *Monsieur le mécanicien* for the entire teaching profession (imported from France). I was pigeonholed. To them, I had been classified as a low, low proletarian of the laboring class, with everything demeaning that this

33

condition implied to the self-appointed intellectual elite! In other words, I was a blue-collar worker unworthy of their company! This, I happily accepted.

But let's go back to Madame Dorita's washing machine. The worn-out belt had just jumped out of the pulley; I put it back in place, tightened it, and gave Madame Dorita instructions to order at least two new belts in Tahiti. The repair would hold until the new parts arrived, maybe in two weeks.

WHILE screwing the machine's back panel in place, I discovered on its right side a varnished wooden chest. It was a large mahogany chest with beautifully dovetailed angle splices, rope handles, and bronze corner protectors and hinges— a chest of a rare craftsmanship rarely seen today. Curious, I rose, looking at the chest. Then I saw the markings on top: a Seabees logo and letters burned into the wood with a branding iron, a navy anchor, and below: "Sgt. Michael Shay, U.S.N.".

I stared fascinated. The chest looked almost new and in perfect condition. The varnish appeared impeccable. Even the bronze fittings were shining. But the inscription and the materials used made me understand that it actually dated back to World War II, and that I was looking at a relic of the American military base that had existed in Bora Bora from 1942 to 1946. I questioned Madame Dorita:

"Wow! What a beautiful chest! To whom does it belong?"

"To my *tane* (man, husband)"

"May I look inside?"

Madame Dorita appeared embarrassed, but, feeling obliged, she went toward a shelf, removed a key from a glass jar, and kneeled on the bare coral floor to open it. Inside, what was revealed was even more astonishing than the immaculate exterior of the chest. Impeccably organized, the entire state-of-the-art electric and manual carpenter's tool kit circa 1940 shone, seemingly as new as the trunk. A large hand drill, a hand planer, an electric saw complete with old-fashioned cloth-covered electric cords and Bakelite plugs, jigsaws of various sizes, a complete set of wood chisels, a brace, drill bits, and other tools were carefully aligned and stacked inside the chest. And everything was well oiled and shone like new.

We were in some sort of a storage shack where all kinds of equipment lay about. None of the other items—old bicycles, tools, broken lawn mowers, and miscellaneous others, most of which were certainly only a few years old—appeared to be the object of any regular maintenance. They all showed severe traces of rusting due to the marine environment. This was why the perfect condition of this splendid and immaculate chest was so amazing.

Why did Jacqui pamper these tools so much? And, above all, why had he never used them? I knew Jacqui as an ever-smiling man who was like most of the Polynesians—carefree, uncomplicated, and without excesses. He worked as a truck driver at the Public Works Department; quite a good job. He would stop over maybe once a week at the Yacht Club to have a beer, which meant that I knew him rather well. He appeared to be like most normal people in this world; a good and honest man who

35

simply tried to enjoy his passage on earth with a minimum of complication and effort. I had a hard time picturing him regularly polishing some old tools stored in some obscure chest for the past 40 years. And even more, ever using them.

After washing my hands, I returned to the kitchen and Madame Dorita to finish my coffee. This chest really puzzled me, and I couldn't help asking her more about it:

"How come Jacqui never uses these tools? They are perfect, of great quality."

"You didn't quite understand me. The chest doesn't belong to Jacqui. It belongs to my *tane*. I'm keeping it for him!"

"Slow down! You lost me! Jacqui is your husband and you have four children, don't you?"

"Yes, but only three of the children are his. My oldest daughter, Purotu, the one who married the deacon of Faanui, is by my first *tane*, Mike. He is an American military man who was stationed here during the war. His unit was called the Seabees. He is the one who gave me the chest to keep it until his return... And I promised."

"Wait a minute. You mean to tell me that you have an American *tane*? That he is supposed to come back and that the chest belongs to him? But I've always known you as Jacqui's wife. Excuse me, I don't want to be too nosy, but I still don't understand very well..."

Madame Dorita remained silent for a while, embarrassed. For the first time in the many years that I had lived on the island, I allowed myself to take a good look at her. She must have been in her late fifties, but her long hair and still slim body made her look quite younger. A few wrinkles on her hands and face were beginning to reveal a life that had had its share of hard work, daily worries, and the burden of the tropical climate. But the still harmonious features of her face suggested that she must have once been of great beauty. However, unlike many beautiful women, especially those who knew that they were, Madame Dorita managed to remain modest, almost shy. This was why this woman—lady would be more appropriate—whom I saw several times a week, never aroused my interest. Until today, she had always appeared to be part of the island's landscape, just as the lagoon or the mountain was. While I felt guilty for not having paid more attention to such a person of quality earlier, she started telling me her story:

"I'm sure you know that the Americans had a Navy base in Bora Bora for almost four years during World War II.

For us people on the island, this event was fantastic. One morning, huge ships suddenly entered the pass. They unloaded trucks, jeeps, houses, canons, pipes, bulldozers, and machines to make electricity; all kinds of things we'd never seen before. And the men who took care of all this were almost all young, handsome, and spoke the language of our first missionaries. The entire population was dazzled by the spectacle. Soon, the island was living a never-ending celebration.

"The school teacher called a meeting between the population and the army people. The population then agreed to lend all the land the Americans needed and, in exchange, they promised to leave the landowners all the buildings and equipment that would remain on the island at the end of the war, when they would leave.

37

"Almost immediately, all the native men on the island worked for the American armed forces. Over the years, the Americans built the docks, the road around the island, the airport on the *motu* (lagoon islet). They installed electricity and water pipes everywhere, as well as huge water tanks and a rainwater collection system in Faanui.

"The island was soon was turned into a real little town with 3,000 soldiers, a power plant, piped water, and even a telephone exchange. Because of security and secrecy, we were sealed off from the rest of Polynesia. We didn't lack anything, food or otherwise; quite to the contrary.

"Although it was forbidden, many families adopted some of the soldiers, the Polynesian way. I was very young at the time the troops arrived, but I still remember how the soldiers used to whistle at me as I walked about with my sisters or my girlfriends. It was only during the base's last year—I had just turned 16—that I became Mike's *vahine*... Imagine, he was a handsome young man, with lots of blond hair, almost red, and he had many soldiers, men working under his command. Their duty was to maintain all of the armed forces buildings on the island. Best of all, he had a Jeep and seemed to be able to obtain all the goods he wanted. He was kind, soft, always stayed close to me, as much as he could, of course, and took good care of my family. We were all so happy.

"Then, one day, the soldiers on the island all seemed worried, thoughtful. They said the Americans had just dropped a terrible bomb on Japan, that thousands and thousands of people had been killed, and that the war was going to end very soon.

"Indeed, three weeks later, there was a great celebration. The fighting was over. The Americans had won. The Japanese had surrendered. But in the village everybody was sad, because we all knew very well that this meant the military would soon leave the island.

"Four months later—by then I was six months pregnant—Mike came to announce that his time to leave Bora Bora had arrived. Two days later, he was to board a freighter that was bunkering at the dock. We both cried a lot, but he promised to return to fetch me, along with the baby. He also gave me his tool chest to keep until his return. We would use it then to build our house. He showed me how to oil the tools, how to wrap the power tools in waxed paper, how to polish and shellac the wooden chest. He explained that I should do it every week, otherwise the sea air would damage and ruin everything. Thus, since that day, every Sunday, after church..."

She paused and took a sip of coffee.

"Once, I almost lost the chest. My daughter Purotu had just been born, and the last American soldiers were leaving the island on airplanes. That's when other soldiers from Tahiti arrived on the trading schooner. Tahitian militiamen called the "Valmy Legion," I think. We called them "blue coats" because of the color of their uniforms. They visited all the houses one by one, and confiscated everything the Americans had left with the families. My father ran home all the way from Vaitape to warn us. While my mother took care of the baby, I carried the chest into the mountains with the help of my older brother. We pulled it all the way up to the foot of the cliff, and hid it in one of the caves where our ancestors used to

39

bury the skulls and bones of the dead. It was a good thing, because when the soldiers from Tahiti came to the house, they took everything else that Mike and other soldiers had given us as presents—even the forks and spoons. Afterwards, an officer came to confiscate all the dollar bills. These soldiers even dismantled the "Quonset huts," you know, the kind of half-moon military building, a former workshop we had next to the house. We were all very sad, angry even, because we had been told that we could keep the Americans' equipment in exchange for the free use of our land. The preacher explained to us later that perhaps the people in Papeete did this in revenge, because during the war, Bora Bora had everything available, while few boats called in at Tahiti and many people were scrambling for food and most basic items. This looting of Bora Bora must have lasted a good year. They even dismantled all of the island's water system and electric lines, starting with the telephone network.

"I left the chest in the cave for at least two years; it was wrapped in copra bags and hidden under some bones. But I went there every other week to grease the tools, discreetly because the militia soldiers knew people were hiding things and kept on searching everywhere. But since the cave area was taboo, they never dared go up there. They were too scared of the *tupapau*, the ghosts. That's how I was able to keep Mike's chest. Now, you understand why many older folks on the island do not like people from Papeete much."

What a story! I could imagine the scene, especially the disappointment of the island's population facing Tahitian authorities who did not respect the agreement that had been signed earlier. I had heard some rumors about what had happened at that time, but Bora Bora people seldom speak of these sad days, proof of the extent to which they must have felt distressed, helpless…and hurt. We remained silent for a while. I broke the spell:

"What about Mike? Did he come back? Did he write to you?"

"Not yet. But he'll be coming soon. He promised, you know… And he is a good man, Mike, he's a fair man. He must have gone to another war, and he hasn't had the time yet. But I'm waiting, he will come back… I know it."

"What about Jacqui in all this? He must know about the chest and everything it means to you, doesn't he?"

"Of course! Actually, Jacqui had always been in love with me. He also knew Mike and, after his departure, he courted me. I refused because I had promised myself to Mike. On my twenty-second birthday, he decided to speak to me in earnest. He explained to me that I was wasting my youth, that I should live with him until Mike came back, and that he promised to set me free as soon as the American returned. I thought a long time about it. My parents were getting old, my daughter needed a father, and I needed to have a man too. So, I accepted his offer. After the birth of the third child, we got married to make everything legal. Jacqui is a wonderful man. He has always been such a very good father to Purotu. And that's the way things have been since… Mike will be coming soon… and Jacqui knows it…"

EIGHT months later, during a flight from Paris to Tahiti, I stopped in Los Angeles. After all my shopping was done and I had visited my rare friends, I found myself with a few free days until the next flight to Tahiti. Madame Dorita's story just kept popping up in my mind. Beautiful love stories are much too rare these days to be unimportant, and this one was equal to any Greek tragedy. Thus I decided to make a visit to the missing persons department of the Veteran's Administration.

There, a young lady with an exaggeratedly hair-sprayed maroon hairdo greeted me. I explained that I was looking for the address of a Michael Shay, a U.S. Navy engineer (Seabees), working in maintenance, who had been stationed from 1944 to 1945 on the island of Bora Bora. She asked for the reason for my inquiry, quoting the right to privacy as spelled out by one of the amendments to the Constitution. Guessing her to be a romantic lady, I simply told her Madame Dorita's story with all its heart-breaking details. I relayed the story in such a moving way that the young woman even started to sob, which jeopardized the perfect balance of her elaborate hairdo. After showing documents proving my residency on the small island lost in the vast South Pacific, she finally agreed to type some coded numbers on the keyboard of a computer. In less than three minutes—Big Brother's world is ever so efficient!—she returned with two pages of printed paper and handed them to me, making me promise to call her so she would know the end of this amazing and touching love story. After a last glance at the printout, she whispered a farewell:

"Don't you go and break a marriage, Promise!"

The information was extensive. Michael Shay had been discharged from the Navy at the end of 1946 after a last six-month stint with the US occupation forces in Nagoya, Japan. Not having known combat, he had not been wounded during his tour of duty. After an honorable discharge, he had applied for a veteran's loan to study engineering for three years at the University of California at San Diego. In 1951, he married a Suzanne North of Albuquerque, New Mexico. Two children were born from this marriage, a girl in 1951 and a boy in 1954. Since that time, he has continuously lived in Río Miñas, a small town 35 miles north of Santa Fe, New Mexico. Mike's phone number was even listed at the bottom of the page.

I called him that evening. I pretended to be a historian doing research on the Pacific War, specializing in US overseas bases. He willingly agreed to meet with me and explained where to find his office.

An early plane to Santa Fe, a rented car, and the next day, around 11 am, I was driving along the Main Street of Río Miñas, a honky town of some 2,000 souls baked by the desert sun, whose only asset appeared to be a street about half a mile long, bordered by stores, and a railroad track with a small station and bare hills as a backdrop. Most of the buildings dated back to the forties and fifties, as if the town had been born in some boom. The hills and valleys in this region were so barren that one could be forgiven for thinking that during Genesis, God somehow forgot to hand out trees to this area. Every store along the road had posts for tying up horses, but today, big pick-up trucks driven by booted cowboys were the new standard. Over half of the businesses along Main Street were either saloons or restaurants. Greasy burger and exhaust fumes and desert dust were the town's subtle perfume. One could feel right away that one was in the South West, with everything that this implied. Indians, Mexicans, and a few blacks living north of the railroad tracks, with Anglos, the whites, living on the other side as was the rule in those days. Washington, its civil rights, and equal opportunity laws were far, far away, and the word "liberal" was surely still considered to be a dirty word in this town. A stranger, of course, had to be suspect, even a bad omen. Judging by the frowns on the faces of the shiftless men in boots and Stetson hats who were sitting idle in the shade on the stores' small patios, their eyes following, one could imagine that some South-Western American traditions were still quite alive down here. This all smelled of Panhandle and boondocks…

"Shay & Son, Contractors" was a one-story frame building at the end of town, identical in style to all other buildings fronting the dusty main street. Two large air conditioners were attached to the window openings, buzzing and drooling like a couple of prehistoric insects. A Lincoln Continental and two pick-up trucks with guns in the rack were parked in front of the entrance. A steer's skull with two huge horns decorated the space above the door. Seen from the outside, the business looked like it must have known better times. The town's resources were a few cattle and, essentially, the nearby uranium mines. The construction business was closely tied to the economic health of the atomic minerals industry. The anti-nuclear energy campaigns of the seventies seemed to have left a deep economic brand on the area, one reason this town in a gun-loving macho country would not give a very warm welcome to any bearded and long-haired hippy. I thanked the Lord for having made me visit the barbershop.

Inside "Shay & Son," one entered through the secretaries' area. On the right sat a smiling aged lady, probably the bookkeeper, and on the left, a petite blonde in her thirties with super-platinum hair, artificially colored of course. Her body was shaped like a pear in a way that I had rarely seen: her torso was tiny but her hips were enormous. At the end of the huge room full of filing cabinets, coffee machines, desks, and a Xerox copier was a kind of a glass cage: the boss's office.

THUS I finally found myself facing Mike, this wonderful ex-Navy sergeant for whom Madame Dorita had been waiting these past thirty years. He was now a rather heavy man, almost bald, with only a bit of gray hair on each side of his cranium; but strong and jovial. He greeted me warmly with a strong Southern drawl, Texas style. He was wearing the unavoidable cowboy boots, a beautiful white Mexican shirt with a string held by a silver dollar in place of a tie. He greeted me warmly and respectfully, certainly impressed by the phony credentials I had given on the phone. He was obviously one of the small town's dignitaries, a pillar of his ailing community.

I felt right away that he wanted to talk. Like most men of his generation, it was evident that he loved to tell it all about "his" war, which was also his youth. He had prepared a few documents after my phone call the previous night—his military records and some photographs—but these only showed groups of men in uniforms, all taken in Japan during the occupation. Not a photograph taken on Bora Bora was in the lot. Impressed by the distance I had traveled just to meet him, he invited me for lunch in a restaurant in the next town where, he explained, "they serve what you call a real steak." We drove in his air-conditioned Lincoln Continental. It was 20 miles to the announced eatery, a fancy steak house decorated Western style with steer horns over the door, saddles, ropes, a mechanical bull, and all the usual overdone cowboy adornments inside.

As we were eating our way through pieces of barbecued meat the size of toilet lids, Mike spoke slowly about his wartime adventures and experiences. I just let him talk, pretending to take notes. I questioned him mostly about his stay on Bora Bora. He was a natural observer, very detail-oriented, and thus revealed a maze of unknown trivia, precise information concerning the naval base operation, sometimes in direct contradiction with the stories that the natives today tell about that time. He talked for two hours, two long hours of details and anecdotes on military life on the South Sea Islands; but never once did he mention Madame Dorita. The only woman he actually spoke of was Eleanor Roosevelt, the President's wife, who had stopped over to visit the Bora Bora base on a return trip from Australia and New Zealand.

I found Mike to be intelligent and very much in tune with his Southwestern environment; even so, he sometimes exaggerated a little bit in his tales. But this must just be a natural trait of the area.

After dessert—some enormous ice creams—I dared drop my little question:

"What about the Bora Bora *vahines*? How did things go with them?"

He looked me straight in the eyes for a while. I remained poker-faced. He then gazed around the dining room to make sure no one could hear, leaned toward me, and almost whispered:

""Yes Sir, I just knew you was gonna ask me that question. Many people used to be quite curious about them things thirty some years ago, when the movie *South Pacific* was the big thing... To you, I'll tell the truth. I've got to admit you're really the first one to hear this, but I have to confess. This must remain a secret between us... You and I are true gentlemen, of course... I know I can trust you...

He quickly looked around the room again.

"Yes, you bet! I had myself one of them little island girls over there. A real cutie. Just as I had a little Jap girl, later on in Nagoya. They were nice, real nice, I'd say... You've got to understand that even us, Southern men, are sometimes attracted by colored women, especially when you ain't got nothing else around... You see what I mean, don't you?..."

With a big grin on his face, he gave me a wink with his left eye and started to laugh loudly... maybe in relief that he had at last told someone.

Mike had been right to trust me. I never told anyone about this trip to New Mexico.

And as far as I know, Madame Dorita continues, as always, after church, to grease and shine Mike's tools in the big, beautiful wooden chest...

Historical note: According to military records, during WWII some 4,400 American G.I.s were based on Bora Bora at one time or another. Local records show that they fathered 132 children with Bora Bora girls. Only a single one of these soldiers, a radio operator, came back to get his *vahine* and marry her. This was quite a feat as, using tough visa restrictions that were applied until the late 1950s, the French authorities had used all legal and bureaucratic means to prevent former US military personnel from returning to the islands.

A little Problem
at the End of the World

ALETTER was waiting for me when I returned from a trip to the island of Huahine. "It is from the minister!" said my *vahine* (Polynesian wife), smiling and excited. A quick kiss to the family and I read the letter. It was just a little note asking me to come and see him, as he might have an assignment for me.

Two days later, on the island of Tahiti, I was in the government building in a quiet, posh, air-conditioned office, sitting opposite the minister, also a longtime friend. The stylish and cozy leather armchair that supported my buttocks represented at least three months of my modest income. But the kindness of my host, the slight embarrassment that he showed in receiving me in such luxurious quarters installed by a predecessor, quickly made me understand that my friend had managed to re-sist the corrupting and intoxicating forces that power often induces. He was now quite popular for having sold the big ministerial limousine and continued to travel on his Italian scooter. But he had it painted black: "It looks more high class!"

He explained the reason for my presence:

- "Well, I want you to go to Takareva. We received a letter from the chief of the atoll. He seems very worried. There appears to be a problem with the lagoon. It does not go into details. He only speaks of dead coral.

"I heard that you've just finished a study on a similar problem. Maybe this will be a similar case. If there is problem, I just can't see any possible source of pollution. Takareva is a small atoll with a lagoon totally enclosed by a fringing reef, and is one of the most isolated islands on the planet... There is another specific reason why I chose you to go. You see, the people on the atoll are part of those communities still steeped in tradition, such as is the case on the islands of Rapa Iti or Maiao. If I send one of my scientists there, he'll dazzle the population with scientific words and no one will understand anything; but even so, they all will say that they do out of respect and politeness. You at least know how to describe complex things using simple words. And above all, you under-stand the mentality of the islanders.

"So please, go to Takareva to see what is happening there. You always tell me that you love atolls. Here is one that really is at the end of the world. Give me your re-port after you return."

Full of joy, I left the office of my minister friend. I was happy to return to the islands, especially to an atoll 1200 kilometers from Papeete…far away, thus authentic. The longer the distance from Tahiti, the more the reflexes are still Polynesian, the more people radiate kindness, the more I feel lucky to be able to go to these islands.

It took me almost three weeks to reach Takareva. Two weeks to wait for the next Air Tahiti flight to the Eastern Tuamotu Archipelago. The airplane was an old De Havilland Twin Otter, a short take off and landing bush plane that was admirably well suited for the short airstrips on coral atolls.

There were no tourists on the plane. And with good reason. It is a bi-monthly flight, so the visitor has a choice between spending an hour or two weeks on any of the atolls along this air route.

As usual, I found myself squeezed between a voluminous but happy Polynesian lady and portable coolers or huge bags full of fresh French bread stored in the aisle. My friend Coquet, a veteran island pilot, was at the controls. Despite his habit of always performing a sign of the cross just before takeoff, a very reassuring gesture for the passengers who could see him because the door to the cockpit had been removed, I knew him as one of the best pilots of French Polynesia. He had made a royal demonstration during a medical evacuation to Tetiaroa that involved landing on a dark, moonless night on a short air strip with its limits miserably lit by a few coconut leaf bonfires.

We made short stopovers on the atolls of Anaa and Makemo and a longer one on Hao to take on additional fuel. Only five hours after leaving Papeete, my friend Co-

quet left me standing in the strong noon sun at the edge
of the blinding white coral runway on the atoll of Tangatepipi.

The postman of the atoll was waiting for me. I was the
only passenger to step off the plane. He was responsible
for driving me in his *kau* (local outboard speedboat) to
Takareva because this atoll had no landing strip. The entire population of the island was also present to assist the
bimonthly aircraft visit. It is always a great event because
the plane brings the mail, "urgent" goods, and some fresh
bread. Sixty *Paumotus* (Tuamotu natives) sat on the sand
in the shade of a large *kahaia,* a kind of balsa tree. The
arriving mail was distributed in silence immediately after
the plane had taken off. As everybody knew each other in
this small community, there was no need to call names.

The *mara'amu*, the strong Southeastern tradewind, had
started blowing the day before my arrival, and was building huge swells on the great ocean. Thus we had to wait
five days before we could safely venture out of the lagoon; five days of vacation during which I accompanied
the postman who visited his small pearl farm and col-
lected wild terns eggs, as the laying season was underway. My new friend explained to me the *paumotu*
method of collecting the eggs, a method that ensures
avoidance of waste. Here's how it's done:

Each atoll generally has one or two uninhabited *motus*
(islets) or sandbars where seabirds lay thousands of eggs
side by side. Should you pick them randomly, most
would be partly hatched, thus inedible and to be thrown
away. To avoid this, while taking care not to crush any
egg, you trace a triangle with a piece of twine, its cor-

ners wedged under blocks of coral, or simply draw lines in the sand with a piece of wood. Then you very carefully move all the eggs that are within that triangle to the outside, taking care to leave enough space between them to allow their mothers to hatch them. You have to be careful not to turn the eggs while moving them because the chick within could suffer. Then you just have to come back the next morning and each of the following days to collect the eggs that are then inside the triangle. They are guaranteed to be fresh because they have been laid during the previous night. These fresh eggs have a strong taste of fish, but I like fish omelet, like all *Paumotus* do.

I also used the imposed stay to do some diving in the colors of the enchanting underwater world of a Tuamotu lagoon. What a pleasure to rediscover the thousands of different hues of the corals and gorgonians. What a joy to be dazzled by the metallic colors of the *pahua* lips, the tridachnae clams whose giant clamshells are pink instead of white in some islands. What happiness to become a participant in a fairy ballet of swarms of fish of all colors and kinds.

Blue and green parrotfish were waiting for me, with their large lips, as if they all wanted to give me a big kiss. A moray eel showed me her long teeth at the entrance to her cave. A clown fish stopped just in front of my mask and tried to hypnotize me with her big round eyes, vigorously shaking her small pectoral fins. A tiger ray made an elegant demonstration of her art of gliding. Even the quiet and scornful passing of a large black-tipped shark seemed to confirm that everything was normal in this beautiful, silent world of color. Diving among these peaceful fish felt like a reunion with some good old buddies from other lagoons; their curiosity, their familiarity, their ballet almost made me believe that they recognized me.

The wind had calmed down. It took us seven hours to reach the atoll of Takareva, located some 40 miles to the northeast of Tangatepipi. The sea was still choppy and confused. Seven hours of ocean spray in the face. Seven hours spent clinging to the dashboard of the *kau*, which jumped from one wave to the next. Seven hours of torture, bending my knees to absorb the shock of the boat landing on the following wave.

Dead tired, burned by salt and sun, it was only in the afternoon that we entered the small pass in the Takareva barrier reef. Then, suddenly, everything became calm. Now navigating inside the small lagoon was like sailing in a bathtub. The main *motu* appeared to our right. At its closest point, almost on the beach, a small white church, topped with a red roof and a pointed steeple, stood proudly. We approached the village while zigzagging between the coral patches. The dwellings, a dozen houses, were now appearing on each side of the religious building, its bell ringing to announce our arrival.

The population stood on the beach where we landed the *kau*. The postman kissed everyone while I shook hands with twenty men and children, and had my turn to give a kiss to all the fifteen women living on the atoll.

My companion the postman distributed the few letters that he had brought along. The head of the island guided me to the house where I was to stay. Of course, he had given me his own bedroom. First, I refused because I could already imagine him sleeping with his wife on mattresses on the floor. But due to his insistence, I had to accept. The laws of Polynesian hospitality are such.

The room was furnished with a four-poster bed covered with a beautiful *tifaifai* (Tahitian quilt) and protected by a large mosquito net. In one corner, stood a table decorated with small multicolored cushions. A large part of the wall was covered with dozens of yellowing photographs. Pictures of weddings. Portraits of babies. A Polynesian in a French army uniform. Girls smiling. A pilgrimage procession. A group of smiling people posing in front of the cathedral of Papeete. To the left of the photos, a small frame showing a grade school diploma issued in Rangiroa. The summary showing the pride of a simple, modest Christian family who lived between the stars and the ocean spanned the wall covered with white-washed coral lime. All the memories of a family forgotten at the end of the world, lovely and beautiful people with a big, big heart.

After a quick dinner consisting of fried fish and *uto*, the sweet inside of sprouted coconuts that looks a bit like a sponge and which is sometimes nicknamed "the bread of atolls." Bone tired, I quickly crashed into bed and went to sleep.

The next morning, after a short prayer, the head of the island, a young boy, and myself took an outrigger canoe to go dive in the lagoon. The old chief had not lied. Almost all the coral in the Takareva lagoon was dead. The great underwater coral mounts, which usually showed an explosion of magical colors, were now just sad brown and gray castle ruins. All the fragile limestone was covered with some slimy and repulsive gray algae. Gone were the red or blue gorgonian fans. Not a single patch of blue coral. Even the large pearl shells were just ugly dishes, their mouths wide open, as if they had died while attempting a last cry of distress. On the sandy bottom, thousands of shells, cones, as well as cowries were scattered, just as dead and covered with algae.

We dove all day in this immense sadness, in this marine necropolis. Throughout the lagoon, the desolation was the same everywhere, the slimy algae covering the skeletons of a previously stunning wildlife. The only species that seemed to survive were large tridachnae clams and a variety of green coral fire. And the fish, of course. They were still there, although far fewer. But they seemed nervous, frightened, traumatized by the cataclysmic upheaval of the environment that had been their paradise for millions of years.

The following day, we made other dives into the ocean, outside the barrier reef, all around the atoll. Here, everything was blooming life, everything was color, everything was magic, everything was normal. Thus, it was only the lagoon that had suffered a mortal blow. Yes, here was the same phenomenon that had struck Suvarov atoll and other coral islands of the Pacific and the Indian Oceans. It would not be easy nor pleasant to explain it to these brave atoll people, these innocent people.

THE MEETING took place that evening, on the beach, around a bonfire. The entire small community was there, sitting on *peues* (woven pandanus mats). Many children had already fallen asleep on the laps of their mothers, while others were sleeping on mats, often next to their dog. A horizontal half-moon crescent was suspended in the Western night sky among the stars, and was reflected as a white stripe on the lagoon.

The chief was standing at my side to translate into the *paumotu* dialect when necessary. I was sad and embarrassed. I hated to be the bearer of bad news:

"Hmm... There... Yes, almost all of your lagoon coral has died. Unfortunately, your atoll is not the only one to have this problem. It is the sad fate of many small, totally encircled, and shallow lagoons across the tropical Pacific Ocean. I will try to explain. The problem is quite complicated. So please be patient. If you have any questions, feel free to interrupt me."

I saw every eyebrow being raised, the Polynesian way to say yes.

"Our planet, our world, is undergoing a climate change. You should have noticed signs of this change. The 1983 and 1992 hurricanes are only the most visible parts. The regular and fragile cycle of seasons is being disrupted. And many people around the world are affected by this phenomenon. We have rainy seasons disturbed, more hurricanes, and periods of unusual warmth. Africa suffers droughts that kill millions of people. While torrential rains create rivers of mud that bury whole towns in South America. Harvests in North America burn in drought while those in Europe are rotting in the rain. The climate around the world has gone haywire.

"Unfortunately, these beautiful atolls where you live are also the most fragile environment of our globe. You live on a strip of sand and coral that emerges on average

57

one and a half meters, five feet, above sea level. An ocean
that is 18.000 km wide and just as long. One and a half
meters in 18.000 km. It's like a slim sheet of paper in the
middle of your lagoon, which is six kilometers in diam-
eter. In addition, the atoll is protected by the barrier reef
that is a living bulwark. It consists of billions of small
polyps that secrete new limestone as fast as the atoll is
sinking into the vastness of the Pacific.

"Thus, as your little island is the most fragile environment, it is unavoidable for it to be the first affected by
climate change. The proof is here. Your lagoon is dead."

"But how did it die?" the chief asked.

"For the moment, the only lagoons that are severely affected are small, shallow, and enclosed lagoons that do
not have a large pass. Like yours. Let me try to explain.

"Since 1982, the normal trade winds and currents in the
Pacific change periodically. This happened occasionally
in the past. It's called the 'El Niño' and 'La Niña', and
they may last a few months, even a year. But since 1982,
this anomaly is almost permanent. And that's what killed
your lagoon—the trade winds blowing from east to west
across the Pacific have disappeared. They even sometimes become western winds. The normal trade winds
create constant cyclical waves that lift water from the
colder depths to the surface. This is called 'up-welling.'
Also, the regular trade winds push more water to the
west, helped by the large Humboldt Current that brings
cold water from Antarctica to our latitudes. But when
there are fewer trade winds, there is also less cold current.
The sea then gets dramatically warmer. That is what creates favorable conditions for hurricanes.

"But also less wind means much less swell. Fewer large waves that break on the reef and ensure that water in the lagoon is constantly renewed and oxygenated. Sometimes even a whole month can pass without a single wave breaking over the barrier reef. And the level of the ocean drops in the central Pacific. Up to 40 centimeters below normal levels, in some areas.

"Because the usual currents and constant trade winds push so much water westward, the central Pacific sea level is slightly higher than it is along the American coast. So we have a warm sea, added to a low sea level, and little or no waves, which normally renew the water inside the lagoon. The lagoon is separated from the surrounding ocean. The lagoon water gets warm, which will deplete the oxygen it contains even faster. And the sun heats all this up even more. Under these extreme conditions, it can take only a few weeks to raise the water temperature over 35 degrees Celsius. That's what kills all the coral. The coral is boiled, it also suffocates, all the way to the bottom of the lagoon. Everything is cooked. Small lagoons heat quickly and their oxygen is rapidly depleted, just as is the case in small pans. The large and deep lagoons with multiple passes take years to heat. That is why Tangatepipi's lagoon has not been affected."

Everyone was silent. Then the leader broke the silence:

"Yes, you're right. I remember diving often in hot water, too hot. We discussed it among ourselves. Also, for a long time, the level of the lagoon was very low, and the barrier reef and the coral heads inside the lagoon were sticking out of the water." All the men now remembered, and a long conversation ensued between them. Then the chief repeated:

"Yes, yes, you're right. But you do not explain why the climate changes. Are things going to get back to normal?"

"Unfortunately, I do not think so. This could even become worse. That's what famous scientists think."

"But why? Is it our fault?"

Beautiful people. This reflex that always drives Polynesians to feel responsible for all ills. This time again, the small community at the end of the world was just an innocent victim.

"This certainly is not your fault, be reassured. There are two culprits responsible for the climate change: carbon dioxide and chlorofluorocarbon, CFC. Wait, let me explain.

"Carbon dioxide has always been a part of the air we breathe. But the advent of modern technology has seriously increased the percentage of this gas in the atmosphere. Modern society depends on mechanical energy to replace the hard work formerly carried out by man or animal. Work such as moving, carrying, digging, pushing, manufacturing, heating, cooling.

"All this energy is mainly produced by combustion engines, automobile engines, and large power stations. These are the engines that emit excess carbon dioxide because they burn fossil fuels; especially the hundreds of millions of cars in the world. So much so that in just these last 30 years, the rate of carbon dioxide in the atmosphere has increased by 10%! The more the air contains that gas, the more it retains the sun's heat, and the warmer our atmosphere gets, and the more the climate changes. This is called the 'greenhouse effect.'

"And the other gas, chloro-something, is a chemical gas that was invented by man seventy years ago to run refrigerators. Unfortunately, he soon found other ways to use it, such as spray cans and air conditioning. This gas destroys the protective ozone layer on the top of the atmosphere. The same layer that stops the ultraviolet rays, the harmful rays of the sun. So these rays begin to penetrate the atmosphere and more heat is absorbed by the carbon dioxide. And the climate changes even more."

They all remained silent. I saw that my friends had not understood. One must realize that this atoll has no spray can, no car, no air conditioner. I thus had to explain in depth:

"An air conditioner is a refrigerator for people. When it's hot, people in cities switch on this machine to cool their homes. This machine consumes a lot of energy, so it sends a lot of carbon dioxide into the air. It is quite expensive, but these people have a lot of money to waste.

"But there is worse yet. In America and Europe, most people live in a cold climate. They work hard and all dream of living in a warm climate like Florida, Arizona, or the French Riviera. One day, they manage to move to these areas. But, instead of enjoying the hot weather, they immediately install air conditioners to recreate at great expense the cold climate they just left. Even their cars and their workplaces are equipped with these machines. They love the cold so much one wonders why they ever moved to hot countries.

"This bizarre behavior of hundreds of millions of people has created an entire industry that generates millions and millions of air conditioners each year. And all these machines are bound to have a gas leak, and then sooner or later end up in a trash pile. Their gas has escaped into the atmosphere and will further reduce the ozone layer. And the climate will change even more."

Everyone looked at me with big eyes. The leader spoke:

"Is your story true? Or you are making fun of us?"

"I'm not making fun. It is unfortunately true. Too true. But I must explain aerosol cans. They contain the same gas, but not for the cold. It is just wasted to spurt products; generally totally unnecessary.

"In former times, when a woman wanted to spray some *monoi pipi* (perfume) on herself, she used a bottle with a small rubber ball at one end. Pffft, pffft, she pushed a couple times on the rubber ball, it vaporized the perfume, and she smelled good. But it was too tiring to push twice on the rubber ball. So modern man invented the aerosol can on which you only have to press once. It destroys the ozone layer, but that doesn't matter. The delightful little finger is not tired. That's what is important.

"And as civilized people love to buy these aerosols, they put almost everything in this type of package: paint, polish for furniture, foam for shaving, a product to smell good under the arm, a product so their toilets smell good. Cream to put on cakes. Starch for ironing. Lacquer to keep hair in place. All things that could be sprayed or dispensed without gas."

My listeners were dismayed now. A murmur was traveling within the small group.

The chief spoke:

"Are you trying to tell us that our lagoon is dead because *Popaas* (foreigners) want to be cold, do not want to tire their little finger, and want their toilets to smell like perfume?"

"Yes, but it is not only *Popaas*. This happens in every city around the world. Even on Tahiti, especially in Papeete, where you see many palaces built for the government, city hall, and so forth. And they all are air-conditioned. Some buildings do not even have a window that can be opened. For one hundred and fifty years, the open window or an electric fan had been enough. But now the public servants cannot work if their offices are not air-conditioned. Even the cars are more and more air-conditioned. They call it progress. Ah, and the cars! Everyone wants a car. You're not a man without a car. There are only 130 kilometers of roads in Tahiti, but they import 20 kilometers of cars each year."

"Thus, the most incredible nonsense has taken place. In Tahiti, on this small rock lost in the middle of the ocean, people who do not know anymore how to walk a few hundred yards, and want to adopt the lifestyle of major industrialized countries, are trapped in monstrous traffic jams. And that happens just a few kilometers from calm coconut groves and placid lagoons.

"No, this is not a matter concerning only *Popaas*. Perhaps your cousin, even your brother, is currently traveling in an air-conditioned car to quickly return to his air-conditioned home. And this is what helps to kill your lagoon. Something strange, maybe some virus, makes people go crazy when they live in a town. They turn into beings that always want more gadgets, always have to have another toy, have to possess the same fashionable things as their neighbor. They have acquired an inexhaustible hunger for mostly useless objects. That's what kills your lagoon.

"Responsible for your dead lagoon are carbon dioxide and CFC. But the real culprits are the people who live in the cities."

"But the leaders of the major cities, do they know that their people are killing our lagoon, our fish? You're going to tell them, aren't you?"

"Of course they know. They've known for many years."

"Really! They then must have banned air conditioners, sprays and unnecessary cars?"

"Alas, none of that. They still hold meetings and large debates in air-conditioned halls; thousands of scientists from around the world. They decided to reduce production of CFC gases by half in the next thirty years. No, no, I'm not kidding.

"One country, one, the United States, banned the sale of spray cans containing CFCs on its territory thirty years ago. But it still exports aerosols that contain CFC gas to other countries.

"For cars, nothing has been changed. Quite the contrary. Last year, the governments of all industrialized countries proudly announced that their factories produced millions of cars more than the previous year. Car emissions of carbon dioxide into the atmosphere are increasing every year. To further affect the climate. To better kill your lagoon."

Appalled, the old chief looked at me. After a long pause, he could say a few words:

"But these people have gone mad! How about us? And our lagoon?"

"Unfortunately, you are only a few hundred atolls, with a few thousand people. So you have no weight. No influence over the millions of people living in cities manufacturing, distributing, and selling all those spray cans, air conditioners, and cars. Governments get their revenues from these industries. They surely do not want to kill the goose that lays the golden egg. It is these same governments that have the largest number of big cars and large air-conditioned palaces. Just look at what is happening in Tahiti.

"No measures will be seriously undertaken to protect the environment as long as the climate imbalance does not radically affect the way of life in the big cities. And knowing them, if the climate warming continues, they will simply install more powerful air conditioners. If the air is polluted, they'll wear masks, as it already happens in major cities like Tokyo or Shanghai. For them, happiness is driving a two-ton car powered by a huge V8 engine 200 yards to the grocery store to buy a loaf of bread. When a nuclear power plant explodes and the radioactive cloud passes over Europe or Japan, almost nobody complains. These people are willing to accept almost anything, as long as they regularly get a new trinket, and as long as the television programs entertain them.

"You, on this atoll, you live in harmony with nature because you have to. Yet the city dude, he doesn't know nature anymore. He wants an artificial climate. Go look at the buildings in the cities, some have no window you can open. He prefers artificial light, neon. He does not want his foot to touch the earth that feeds him. To him, it is only dirty mud that would soil his shiny, expensive shoes. Thus, he paves with concrete every square inch. If a 300-

65

year-old tree that offered shade and fruits to generations might cause motorists to slow down a bit, it will be cut without the slightest remorse. It is 'move over! Progress is on its way. Whole forests disappear, millions of square kilometers, since they are not considered 'productive.' Yet they are the ones that absorb carbon dioxide and provide oxygen to our planet. But one cannot sell the oxygen, so it is not 'profitable.' Thus they are replaced with crops that have a market value.

"Yes, your lagoon is affected by what happens in big cities, even those on the other side of the world. And indeed your lagoon is one of the first victims of the madness of men of our times. There will be many other victims, some quite unexpected. People in the cities eradicated hunger a long time ago—or so they believe... time will tell. All the gadgets of the industrial world have become a necessity for them, just as a mother's womb is necessary for a baby's survival. The gadgets are now their comforters; they represent security. Even so, the city people seem arrogant; they are actually living in constant terror of losing their little toys. In fact, they are merely poor puppets suffering from an insecurity syndrome that you, living here on your isolated atoll, cannot even begin to imagine."

THREE weeks later, I found myself facing my friend the minister in his air-conditioned office in the large building without windows. Though being a Tahitian, he looked pale. Decidedly, neon lights do not give a tan.

I resumed the story of my sad journey.

He remained silent while looking at me. He was thinking.

After a quarter of an hour, it was me who broke the silence:

"Hmm ... And I have not told all to the people of Takareva."

"Ah? What more is there to tell?"

This time, it was my turn to remain silent for one minute.

"Two things. The first concerns the fish, their staple food. The lagoon is now full of dead coral. It is the ideal habitat for small green algae called ciguatoxin. It gives ciguatera to the fish that eat it. If one of these algae enters the lagoon, it will proliferate. Then the entire food chain in the lagoon will be affected with this poison. And in ten years, no more lagoon fish will be edible. All will be poisonous. That's what happened to the fish of Palmyra atoll, Wake Island, Canton Island, Christmas Island, and Mangareva. All these islands had been dredged during and after World War II, which killed many corals. Sixty years later, you still cannot eat the fish there.

"And there is also the problem of the sea level. Our planet is getting warmer. Water, just as metal, increases in volume when it is heated. And the ice at the poles. It will melt. The water will go into the sea. These two factors will raise ocean levels. Scientists disagree on the extent of the increase. The most optimistic talk of a meter in one hundred years. The more pessimistic speak of three meters. But a meter is more than enough to make the atolls uninhabitable. Fifty centimeters is enough to destroy the freshwater tables at the center of the *motus*."

My friend began to get angry:

"And what else do your damned scientists say?"

"That there are only two points on which they agree: First, for the first time in the history of the planet, humans have managed to modify the climate... And that the changes underway are irreversible."

I left the office thinking it would be wise to stay at a distance for some time...

Editor's note: This story was first written in 1989, at a time when the communist block still existed, and when concerns about climate change were still considered to be "hippy hysteria." In 1994, when Tanner Verlag in Zurich published the German language translation of this book, the literary critic of the very serious German *Frankfurter Allgemeine Zeitung* qualified this short story as "unbelievable non-sense."

You have to deserve
the Marquesan Islands

AREN'T you tired of being a dumb and obedient
tourist who always follows paths predefined by
some obscure travel agent who brags about
places he has certainly never been to? What pleasure is
there in rushing far away to some fashionable place, only
to discover your next-door neighbor has booked the same
tour, even to the middle of Africa? Are you ready for something different? For true, exotic adventure? If your answer
is yes, then there is an unusual, little known escape: The
cruise to the Marquesas on the schooner *Aranui*.

Once a month, the *Aranui* leaves Tahiti for a round trip to
the Marquesas Archipelago. This ship is a "mixed cargo,"
carrying both passengers and merchandise, as almost all
ocean-going ships used to do forty or more years ago. The
cruise lasts two weeks, and the marvelous thing is that on
the outgoing leg of the voyage as well as on the return trip,
the ship calls on various isolated atolls of the Tuamotu, as

well as on all of the Marquesas Islands. The Chinese ship owner was smart enough to provide quality features such as a small pool, stewardesses, even air conditioning for his passengers; a whole universe of luxury unknown on islands still fairly untouched and definitively at the end of the world.

After sailing out the pass through Papeete's barrier reef, a unique companionship establishes itself among the fifty or so passengers, the officers, the stewardesses and the Polynesian crew. The atmosphere is reminiscent of the long gone era of trans-ocean ships when passengers had plenty of time to become interested in each other. Thanks to the *Aranui*'s small size and its calls in remote places, friendliness soon turns into friendship.

A kind of complicity quickly emerges among the various groups sailing on this ship lost between the blue of the sky and the aquamarine blue of the tropical Southern Pacific, because a natural selection of the passengers did take place even before boarding. Indeed, a cruise to the Marquesas Islands will never attract people in search of nightlife, social climbing, fashionable resorts, or another Disneylands. Therefore, most of the first-class passengers are an international blend of experienced travelers, scientists, writers, professional photographers, or romantics, all in search of some Shangri-Las still offering innocence, untouched nature, or solitude. Add to this group some beautiful Polynesian woman with her children on her way to rejoin her husband, a pearl farmer or a school teacher returning to their lost island; a Chinese businessman going to the atolls to buy copra, pearls, or mother of pearl; even one or two French expatriate civil servants, and you'll have a cast of characters worthy of any Jack London or Somerset Maugham novel. Not to be forgotten, of course, are the forty or so deck passengers, mostly Marquesans, Tahitian, and a few European backpackers.

Since a social class structure is not a tradition in our islands, all these people of different backgrounds will soon rub shoulders during the entire trip and, thanks to this concentration of out-of-the-ordinary human beings, the passengers will quickly share their common interests. Any conversation on the deck, in the dining room, or at the bar will prove to be of an intellectual level above the average mediocrity.

A few years ago, my friend Marcel, a well-known photographer who is known to the Tahitians by the nickname "Zizi", a Frenchman who never misses an opportunity to return to our islands, was lucky enough to discover this cruise. All the passengers on board met the above-described criteria... all except for a European lady who stood apart. She was French, with light blond hair, small, and rather skinny. In spite of an apparent obsession with solitude, she seemed quite fragile and pleasant. One would have suspected her to be around forty. Above all, her eyes were fascinating because of the sadness they expressed. Guessing some deep sorrow in her past life, the other passengers somehow felt it was their duty to invite her to share their joyful moments, their shipboard games, and their discovery of the atolls, these "islands full of water." But the lady seemed to prefer to dwindle in some sort of lonely melancholy and, after two days of efforts to make her feel welcome within the group had failed, the passengers scrupulously respected her quest for solitude. Yet, the lady's secret and insistence on loneliness had actually aroused everyone's interest even more. Somehow a passenger managed to find out her name, Christine, but nothing else transpired.

One week after the departure from Papeete, during the call at the village of Atuona on the island of Hiva Oa, the first rainfalls of the season made their appearance. Marcel was upset because he was there mostly to photograph and film Paul Gauguin's as well as Jacques Brel's* tombs, located in the small island cemetery. Seeing the tropical showers, the skipper invited all the passengers to the village's little café so they could taste the delicious and abundant local lobsters, thus cheering them up until the rain would pass. They all accepted with joy and delight. That means all, except for Marcel, who insisted on taking his shots before noon when the light was better. Clad in a raincoat, he hiked the steep trail leading to the little cemetery overlooking the bay. Up there on the promontory, while setting up his tripods and other equipment, the sky suddenly cleared and, under a triumphant sun, the breathtaking view of the large Atuona Bay unveiled itself in all its splendor. Happy and pointing his cameras toward Paul Gauguin's tomb, Marcel felt a presence on his right side. It was Christine passing through the cemetery gate, a small package in her hand, then quickly disappearing from sight.

An hour later, after having taken pictures of Paul Gauguin's tomb from every angle, Marcel moved his equipment to Jacques Brel's gravesite, located some fifty yards further on. That's when he again saw Christine, in front of

---

* **Jacques BREL**, Belgian-born singer, poet, and songwriter, is famous throughout the French-speaking world for the impressionist quality of his songs. Although he also acted in some French movies, he is better known on the American music scene as the author of the song "If you go away" (*Ne me quitte pas*) and his work was celebrated in a Broadway musical *"Jacques Brel is Alive and Well in Paris"*. In 1978, Jacques Brel died of cancer at the age of 49 after having chosen to spend his last years on Hiva Oa, in the Marquesan islands, an archipelago he discovered while sailing around the world on his motorsailer, the yacht *Asgoy*.

that tomb. At the foot of the tombstone, a huge granite monolith carved with the singer's profile and —God only knows why— that of his still-living West Indian female companion, a few fresh, blood-red hibiscus flowers had been placed around a small pink picture frame. Christine seemed embarrassed and dared not look at Marcel. He engaged the conversation:

"Did you place that frame there?"

"Hmm... Yes, I did..."

"Do you mind if I look at it?"

"No… no… not at all... Go ahead!"

He kneeled in front of the tombstone and delicately picked the object up. It was a cheap plastic frame with rhinestone flakes glued to it, the kind one would find just about anywhere in France in dime stores, at carnivals, or around cemeteries. Inside was the picture of a warbler with a poem printed in cursive writing:

> *"Warbling bird,*
> *If you fly*
> *Around this tomb*
> *Sing for him*
> *Your most beautiful song."*

After he had delicately returned the frame to the foot of the tombstone, Marcel realized that Christine had run away.

One hour later, he found her again, sitting in the little café in Atuona. With the sun shining once more, the other passengers had left for the long hike up to the cemetery. Thus Marcel and Christine were alone in the restaurant's small dining room, sitting at separate tables covered with plastic table cloths, waiting silently and motionless for their barbecued lobster to be cooked and brought. She could sense

73

the many questions in Marcel's eyes, which just couldn't stop looking her way. Then Marcel offered to share the bottle of Riesling wine he had just ordered and, surprisingly, she immediately accepted and invited him to move over to her table.

After much uneasiness and exchanging some small talk, she suddenly decided to tell him her story:

"You see, I am a nurse at the big hospital in Nanterre, in the suburbs of Paris. All of my youth was charmed by Jacquot's melodies"—She was talking about Jacques Brel, of course—"I come from a working-class family in a poor suburban Paris neighborhood, and life has always been quite difficult for me. Jacquot with his sad songs quickly became my hero. I must admit that I was in love with him. Oh yes, of course, I knew very well that I was not the only one and that I didn't stand a chance, but it didn't matter. Jacquot and his melodies were my comfort, my life jacket, my secret hiding place in a childhood that had few joyful moments. As you can see, I am not pretty, and my parents' low social status seems to stick to my heels like indelible mud... You might understand why I have been living hidden inside my own shell for so long, like a wounded animal. And deep inside that shell was my Jacquot and his songs."

She paused to sip some wine. Taking a close look at her, Marcel thought it was a shame to see how much damage can be done to someone's life—and mind—by the social class consciousness that is still much alive in Europe. Actually, Christine was quite a beautiful woman, and although her joyless life had branded some hard lines on her face, she seemed to possess all the assets necessary to lead a happy and fulfilled existence.

She delicately returned her glass to the table and went on with her story:

"When Jacquot died so tragically, I felt so sad that I wanted to die. Since I didn't have the courage to jump off a bridge or from the Eiffel Tower, I simply stopped eating. I stopped living. I walked like a sleepwalker. I was slowly letting myself die. Luckily, I work in a hospital, and the first time I fainted, they immediately realized what my problem was. They took care of me, against my will, as I truly wanted to make a smooth exit out of this world. But you know how stubborn they can be in hospitals... So, with lots of medication and quite a bit of psychoanalysis, they managed to bring me back to life—so to speak—after a whole year. Still, I functioned like a robot. Jacquot was and remained my only reason for living and I wanted to be with him. Since they wouldn't allow me to die, I tried to get closer to him by regularly visiting the cemetery at Nanterre and praying. I was praying anywhere inside the cemetery, in front of any grave. It didn't matter which tomb I picked; Jacquot was dead and the cemetery was the land of the dead, that's all that mattered.

"Then one morning on All Saints' Day—God, was it ever cold that morning!—a street merchant had parked his cart at the cemetery's entrance, trying to sell a few funerary gadgets. I was the only person crazy enough to go to the cemetery early that morning, so cold with an icy wind. I took pity on the merchant and I bought the frame you saw... For my Jacquot."

She quickly took another sip of wine to catch her breath.

"That's how I was faced with a dilemma: you can pray anywhere, especially in a cemetery. But you just can't leave a small memento on someone else's grave. Also, this cold, this fog... above all, this sadness... I knew this just didn't

75

have anything to do with my Jacquot. I absolutely had to go to his real grave here in these Marquesas islands he sang so well about, and bring him my little token. I was trapped! My only way out, my only cure, was to come all the way out here and give him my token!

"This happened three years ago. From that moment on, the voyage to the Marquesas became my new obsession. This cheap little plastic frame actually saved my life. Suddenly I had become my reason to live, a purpose in my life. I started saving, depriving myself of everything, living only on the bare necessities, almost on bread and water. Three years of patience so I could gather enough money for the long, long voyage to the Marquesas. Three years to enable me to place this frame here and, at last, pray on my Jacquot's real grave..."

There was a long pause. Marcel remained silent. Christine slowly raised her eyes and, suddenly, started smiling. That smile made her look very different, actually very beautiful.

"Well, now it's done. I can start living... At last!"

And did she ever mean it! As if set free, Christine suddenly looked alive. She started devouring the lobster with an amazing appetite, even emptied the bottle of Riesling without the slightest hesitation or shyness. Marcel immediately ordered another; he understood too well how she must feel...

From that moment on and for the rest of the voyage, Christine became quite a joyful, witty, and attractive companion to the other passengers.

And Christine's deep love for Jacques Brel actually had not been a wasted love. Indeed, during the return voyage, the *Aranui* made its usual call at Takaroa atoll to load copra and unload pearl farm equipment. Bernard, the traveling doctor for the Tuamotu-Gambier health district, took advantage of that stopover to book a passage to Papeete; it was to be a pleasant change from the usual plane trip, and it saved him a three-day wait for the next flight. That evening at dinner, he met Christine and was even more interested in her as soon as he found out that she was also a member of the medical profession.

Four days later, upon landing in Tahiti, a brand new Christine was jumping with joy and showing her happiness to all the passengers. For the first time in her life, destiny had smiled at her. Indeed, thanks to a true coincidence—but was it really a coincidence?—the nursing position on Hiva Oa would become vacant. At the doctor's suggestion, Christine would apply for and be assured of the position as few applicants postulated for jobs in the remote outer islands. To top it all off, because of incentives and compensations, the position offered a much, much higher salary than she would ever earn in France.

At the Papeete dock, while stevedores operated the cranes to unload the thousands of sacs of copra from the *Aranui*, Marcel, cameras and bags hanging off his shoulders, climbed up to the bridge to thank Ako, the ship's second in command who, clad only in shorts and T-shirt, was supervising the unloading. Ako, a Chinese-Polynesian, had been on the Marquesas line for the past twenty years and, as any professional officer should, kept himself well informed of even the most personal aspects of his passengers' business. Leaning on the rail and rolling a cigarette, he greeted Marcel:

"You see, Zizi, the day when Christine came aboard, just looking at her face, I was afraid she might jump overboard some night. That's why I kept a close watch on her... I even had one of my men sleep in front of the door that leads to the passenger cabins...

"That Jacques Brel left us quite a while ago, but this fellow managed to get that woman out of her city dump," he said with a chuckle before continuing, "and he even managed to keep her close to him!

"You see, Zizi, the Marquesan islands, one has to deserve them. Jacques Brel deserved them so well. Everybody liked him because he liked and helped everybody...

"I think Christine is of the same brand... Don't worry about her, she'll be happy there, I'll bet anything on it. People will be kind to her... Have a nice trip. See you next time..."

He lit his cigarette and turned back toward the big open cargo hold.

* *Paumotu*: native of the Tuamotu atolls.

In Search of a Tropical Mate

MARCELLINE is half Chinese, a *Demie-Chinoise*, as we say in Tahiti. That is, her mother is Tahitian and her father Chinese. This blend is fairly common in our islands and often produces the most beautiful girls of Polynesia.

She was born in Faanui, a small fishing village located at the bottom of Bora Bora's large western bay. Her mother named her Marcelline because, at the time she was born, a French gendarme had just been transferred to this end-of-the-world island. His wife was named Marcelline, until then an unknown name on the island, and islanders like new things.

It was a name that didn't bring much luck to the French wife of the expatriate civil servant. The lady had been on the island for less than six months when she boarded the boat for Papeete, the first leg of a hasty but long return voyage to France. The reason for this retreat was that she could no longer stand the competition of Bora Bora's young girls. She decided it would be better to leave the island under the pretext of being unable to adapt to the tropical climate, rather than having to watch her husband succumb to the local female charm. She had resigned herself to wait in France until her husband finished his two-year assignment. It would be a two-year vacation for her and, back home, she could, whenever she wanted, find herself a lover, if only to get even with her husband for all the humiliation she had endured during her six-month stay in the "most beautiful island in the world."

On an island as small as Bora Bora, you just can't keep a secret. It's not that the islanders intend to be cruel, but too often, when she walked by a group of gossiping ladies, she would catch obvious comments such as "Uh-uh, how sad, really, what a pity..."

So, the gendarme's wife discreetly disappeared forever from the small sunny island, without even knowing the true reasons behind the local girls' interest in her husband, a man who, indeed, was neither particularly handsome nor an outstanding stud. Her trouble actually began the day she arrived. Believing herself to be a colonial dame, she had a patronizing and condescending attitude toward the small native community. Thus, to preserve their dignity and regain control of the situation, the proud island folk decided to use their best defense, a never-failing secret weapon: the irresistible seductive power of their girls, especially as no children were involved. The gendarme, a rather colorless law enforcement officer, suddenly became very popular with the local maidens and, from that moment on, his wife's departure from the island was only a matter of time.

Even the French authorities nodded approvingly at this type of evolution because their agent in Bora Bora was now being informed, on the pillow, of all the island's little secrets. The natural order of things had been restored and the small island community could return to its usual tropical lethargy.

But, let's return to the Marcelline, our Tahitian-Chinese beauty. Then aged seventeen, a strikingly beautiful young woman with long black hair flowing in the trade winds, she leisurely pedaled her bicycle along the white coral ribbon circling Bora Bora's main island.

Marcelline was a gorgeous girl of truly exceptional beauty. Her Tahitian mother gave her the strong-boned body and gracefully long hips of the Maori and, above all, a very long neck. She was one of these Polynesian women with a unique attribute seen nowhere else in the world—that of having one more neck vertebra than most common human beings. That long neck gave Marcelline a very distinctive feminine touch and rendered harmonious proportions to her almost masculine body frame. Her silhouette was enhanced by the high and firm breasts of a young woman who hasn't gone through childbirth and breastfeeding; the kind of breasts the Tahitians like to nickname *"pamplemousse"* (grapefruit). Her eyes were almond-shaped and her hair, inherited from her Chinese father, was silky, straight, and charcoal black. Endowed with a pleasant character and truly comfortable with her personality, Marcelline was definitely an outstanding specimen of the female species.

She was then working at the Hotel Taina, a small, somewhat rundown lodge in the village of Vaitape, Bora

Bora's "center." The hotel was on the shore of the lagoon and consisted of some fifteen small bungalows, a bar, and a restaurant, all with *pandanus* (screw pine) thatched roofs. Marcelline was doing a little of everything there: maid, cook, waitress, and receptionist. All of the hotel's employees were young women who all had the same duties—a little of everything. People in our islands remain rather isolated from the complications of formal training, diplomas, and job descriptions.

Marcelline had been trained by Maïte, the senior employee, who explained the mentality of the tourists and taught her how to serve food the Western way. She enjoyed working at the hotel because the staff, in fact, consisted of girls who were good friends and who had fun working together. Benoit, the French manager-plumber-mechanic, was always busy fixing some equipment, especially the small electric power plant. He was smart enough to delegate to the girls the responsibility of running the hotel as they pleased, something they did very cleverly and with loving care, at their own pace. That's how the hotel acquired an excellent reputation for tranquility and authenticity throughout the South Pacific. Just by instinct, the girls had succeeded in creating a small tropical world in perfect harmony with the rhythm of the lagoon's small waves, the kind that tourists crave when they choose to stay in small island hotels.

The girls spent most of their free time decorating the hotel with fresh flowers and woven coconut palms, sweeping the floors, or raking the sand on the beach. The hotel was their entire universe. They spent all of their time there, seven days a week. It would never have occurred to any of them to keep track of their working hours, let alone to punch a time clock. They were content with the way things were and didn't ask for anything more.

Every morning after serving breakfast, they all sat together around a long table in an adjacent room, a large bowl of coffee in front of each one. This was their sacred moment of the day, a time to talk in Tahitian about anything and everything while smoking those little hand-rolled cigarettes that are so popular in Tahiti. It was the moment for exchanging rumors and gossips. Every hotel guest was carefully reviewed and analyzed. They would try, for example, to picture how the couple in bungalow 5 could possibly make love—him being so short and fat while she was so tall and skinny—and wonder aloud whether the tourist in room No. 2 was gay or just shy with women. All of this was, of course, punctuated by loud outbursts of laughter, but never tainted with any mean or malicious thoughts.

ONE morning in June, during the southern winter, a lonely customer showed up at the reception desk of this tiny and tidy female world. He placed his suitcase on the ground and innocently signed the guest register. Little did he know that this signature was about to turn his life upside down!

His name was Horst Werner, a German from Cologne. In his mid-forties, tall, and husky without looking fat, he didn't look his age and had this noticeably elegant look that reflects a familiarity with life's refinements. His forehead was still garnished with light auburn hair, but his pinched nose and bushy eyebrows made him look somewhat stern. He was not what you would call a handsome man, but he was a healthy man radiating stability and tranquility.

Men can usually be divided into three categories:

The first category consists of the young men who seduce women thanks to their stamina and youthful passion: that's called the "shock" effect.

The second category consists of the thirty-five to fifty-year-old men who attract ladies with a sophisticated blend of self-confidence and very expensive clothing: that's called the "chic" effect.

The men in the third category are over fifty years old and generally have only two aces up their sleeves to generate some female excitement: wealth and security. That's called the "check" effect.

Shock, chic, check! It has a good ring to it and is valid in any language, culture or society.

Horst definitively belonged to the second, the "chic" category. He had been a successful man despite a youth traumatized by the horrors of war and growing up as a deprived orphan in post-war Germany. His father had been killed while fighting in Russia and his mother disappeared during one of the numerous bomb raids over the Ruhr industrial region. At age eighteen, without formal training, he became a machine operator in a toilet paper factory. A few years later, the occupying American G.I.s introduced paper handkerchiefs into Germany. Either by intuition or because his mind had not been numbed by too much formal education, Horst was among the first persons to realize that German housewives were ready to pay good money for not having to wash those filthy linen handkerchiefs where germs love to flourish. He also knew that flus and colds were there to stay, especially during those long, harsh German winters.

Twenty years of hard work, persistence, sheer guts, and lots of luck turned Horst into the owner of a company that controlled sixty percent of Germany's toilet paper business. Soon, the gradual widening of the European Economic Community markets brought a new dimension to the consumer goods industry and attracted the interest of multinational corporations. One of these industrial giants made Horst an offer he just couldn't resist; he sold his company and, at age forty, found himself in semi-retirement and forever sheltered from financial worries.

Free of responsibilities and dispensed of daily chores, Horst decided to find himself a wife with whom to share his newly acquired freedom and wealth. His quest started within his homeland where friends introduced him to all kinds of ladies: intellectual ladies, upper-class ladies, perfect housewives, even high-hat nobility ladies. But all attempts to find a mate ended in failure. His dates were certainly willing to marry him the moment they realized the extent of his fortune, but, as soon as they felt confident that the man's heart had been conquered, they all tried to run his life and turn it into a boring routine. Horst, who had been very independent at an early age, found this unbearable and put a quick end to the relationship. None of these ladies was smart enough to put aside her excessive and domineering instinct and this is how one of Germany's most promising eligible bachelors was lost to that country's female league.

After such continuous disappointments, Horst decided to expand his hunting grounds to foreign countries.

In those days, Thailand was a fashionable destination for men of the "Niebelungen Country." Thai women had a reputation for unmatched beauty, femininity, sensuality, and obedience. Following his friends' advice, Horst decided to go there to check it out. His trip to Bangkok turned out to be a disaster.

It took place toward the end of the Viet Nam war, when hundreds of thousands of soldiers on R&R leave had turned the magnificent Asian city into a gigantic whore-house. The buying power of American, Australian, and New Zealand troops had turned Thailand's agricultural economy upside down. During their brief breaks away from "Nam's hell," the G.I.s flew there to indulge in all sorts of rowdiness and to overcome their apocalyptic psychosis. They were spending money like there was no tomorrow. In one night of debauchery with a soldier, a halfway good-looking young girl could earn more cash than a farmer could expect to earn in exchange for six months of painful labor. Thus the streets of Bangkok were swarming with young ladies offering their body for pay. To make things worse, dozens of charter flights were dumping planeloads of European thrill-seekers on this new capital of venereal trade. Any white man alone in Bangkok was automatically perceived as a "John" in search of carnal pleasure. All of the city's activities appeared to be centered on the newfound profitable industry of prostitution with all of its refinements. This, of course, kept any respectable girl at home and off limits to foreigners.

Horst, who had been raised with the rigid values and righteousness of the German middle class, felt quite disgusted by this kind of business. The mere thought of, maybe, at least once just out of curiosity, allowing himself to try one of those Thai "massages" filled him with unbearable feelings of guilt. Like most German men of his generation, he had a very strict and totally inflexible set of moral values. He judged everything and everybody in the whole world according to his merciless German criteria, and he could not for a second consider that, for most of Thailand's young girls, this commerce was the only alternative to a life of hopeless poverty. To him, only respectability mattered.

It is one of the contradictions specific to the Western mind: in order to earn the white man's respect and confidence, the rest of the world must, like him, own all the tangible proof of material success. This is often possible in industrialized developed countries, but in the "Third World," the expensive "civilized man" kit is accessible only to a handful of privileged people.

The worldwide telecommunication explosion and the proliferation of television define and glamorize success as an urban dweller living in a big city universe of microwave ovens, fancy automobiles, and computerized gadgetry. This constant visual assault on the world by American and European TV series has created a new standard of universal values, which is totally incompatible with the resources of overpopulated Third World countries. Young people there are losing respect for their parents and their own communities because they perceive them as social failures. This audiovisual brainwashing accelerates the flight from rural areas, destabilizes traditional food supplies, and creates new urban slums.

The moral and traditional values of agricultural communities, the very cultural fiber of these countries, are threatened by new dangerously shortsighted standards that make them look inferior. Younger generations, who grew up being fed with such models of an easy life, will sooner or later face tremendous frustration when they realize that they can't start dreaming of approaching such standards of living. The Third World is thus shaken by serious chronic social problems arising from its people's inability to share in a way of life that is shown by the media as being commonplace. The recent Islamic fundamentalist movements are but a violent rejection of all Western values appealing to the youth of the poorest Muslim countries. This is just the initial reaction to this frustration; the first movements so far preaching the return to a lost dignity away from the futile race for greedy consumption. Unfortunately, these countries' elite emigrate toward the "Have" societies in order to satisfy their own appetite for material goods. This, for the Third World, amounts to a sad "Marshall Plan" in reverse. With this brain drain, years of costly training to educate managers, doctors, and engineers are being siphoned away, along with these underdeveloped countries' hopes for a better future.

Television sets and video players have become a new colonization weapon much more efficient than the old "battling" machine gun. This show of wealth is just as indecent as eating caviar and drinking Champagne in front of a starving mob. The Western world must soon become aware of the long-term effects of its conspicuous displays of luxury, before frustrated Third World populations become tempted to break the display window to loot the store. This helps us to understand why young girls in Bangkok are so eager to sell their body, just to get a little taste of the "modern" world...

But Horst didn't see it that way; he had nothing but contempt for these girls who, after all, were just reaching for the standards of his own society and had only one commodity with which to pay for them—their own body... How twisted and cruel can our "civilized" world be!

That night, Horst told of his indignation and his great disappointment to an Australian who happened to share his table at the hotel's coffee shop and who was even willing to listen patiently to his laments and boring description of the ideal woman. Amazed by so much self-righteousness and pretension, the Aussie suggested that Horst go try his luck in Manila and convinced him that, among Filipino women, he would be sure to find the rare bird, his model of virtue, beauty, and obedience, a lady who would meet his demanding Teutonic middle-class standards. Unfortunately, Horst didn't catch the ironic smirk on the Australian's face when he wished him "bon voyage" and the best of luck!

Three days later in Manila, Horst was discovering a sad reality of the modern world that he never suspected. The capital city of the Philippines was now a meeting place for perverts, and most of them were Horst's fellow citizens. About everywhere in this large busy city, whenever he revealed his nationality, he was offered young boys for all kinds of depraved sexual games. Never in his life had he felt so ashamed and disgusted. He was horrified by the discovery that his own society, a society he saw as superior and perfect, could produce such sinister deviants who would travel as far as the other side of the world to fulfill, anonymously, their most unspeakable fantasies.

Moreover, the great distance they had traveled suggested that these perversions were certainly not the privilege of some lower social class individuals; much to the contrary. His universe, based until now on the certitude of ethnic superiority and biblical values, was severely shaken. He no longer dared to leave his hotel, perhaps for fear of running into someone from the *Vaterland* whom he would recognize. So he spent his nights getting drunk at the bar. This is how he befriended Boris, the bartender at Manila's Hotel Excelsior...

Boris was in his seventies, his hair white as snow, and he was still exceptionally peppy for a man his age. He was one of the last survivors of a large community of "White Russians" spread all over the Far East, from Shanghai to Perth, from Singapore to Hong Kong. Like their brothers in Europe, these fugitives from Soviet Bolshevism spent over half a century dreaming of the day when they would return to good old Mother Russia; fifty long years of plotting and running exiled governments.

Every large city in the Orient used to have at least one bar with its own "Russian Imperial Government in Exile" and, since their return to power was always thought to be imminent, any serious attempt to take root in the host country or any long-term business venture was perceived to be capitulation or treason by the exiled community. Thus, the quasi totality of Russia's educated elite exiled in the Orient and the Pacific wasted their lives in all kinds of menial jobs: interpreters, hotel concierges, bank or shipping clerks, tour guides, etc. Most of them lived in a permanently temporary universe and were despised by all of their host country's social classes, whether they were native or expatriates.

If anything, the idealism and persistence of this up-rooted generation longing for the return of privileges of a feudal society gone forever, served to confirm one of the lessons of history: it is futile and impossible to bring back "the good old days."

Boris thoroughly experienced this tragic diaspora. At one time, he was even acting as a former "foreign minister in exile" (everyone had the right to be minister at least once!). His many travels—paid, of course, out of his own pocket—to maintain contact between the various exiled communities kept his life exciting; it made him a living encyclopedia who knew each town, each port, and each bar between Colombo and San Francisco.

For two days in a row, Horst tried to drown his sadness at the bar. Boris volunteered to help him empty a few bottles of excellent Australian wine. Shouldn't a good bartender also be like a priest ready to receive confession from any lost soul in search of sympathy and comfort? Over long hours and large quantities of alcohol, Boris listened to Horst's sad stories. After having emptied yet another bottle in order to "clear his mind," he leaned toward Horst and said:

"You know, I am an old man who's done just about everything one can do in one's life... I've been everywhere... I've even caught most tropical and sexual diseases... My life has been one adventure after another, and I have no regrets... except perhaps one: I should have stayed with my Polynesian woman. She was the only woman who ever knew how to give me true rest, peace, and happiness; the only woman who ever appreciated and loved me for what I am: nothing more than a poor unpretentious devil, and basically a good man... She was nothing like many of these white women who are never satisfied with their man and only appreciate what they don't have..."

He took a sip of his wine."It's already been twenty years now since I lived in the Tongan islands with my Polynesian darling. Her name was Salote, just like the former islands' queen; it means Charlotte. She had a magnificent body, long black hair down to her buttocks, like she had jumped out of a Gauguin painting, and, let me tell you, that hair was our only bed cover during the cool Austral winter nights... She had the typical tranquility and pride of Polynesian women, something that cannot be described, that you have to experience for yourself. To top it all, she was hardworking and meticulously clean, as all women are on these islands.

"At the time, I was sailing as a first mate on the *Tiare Taporo*, a big sailing schooner that belonged to the Donald South Seas Trading Company. We traded in copra, mother of pearl, and black pearls between Suva and Papeete. One day, I broke my leg while jumping into the cargo hold. They left me to recover on Vavau, an island in Northern Tonga, until the ship would return. The schooner came back fifteen months later... Fifteen months of total bliss... I never should have left... Today, I would be living somewhere on that tiny island in the middle of the great ocean, with children and grandchildren all around me. But my Russian friends would never have forgiven me; they would have called me a traitor. Now, they're all dead, I'm one of the few survivors and I'm all alone, really alone. You know, when you're getting old, being alone becomes truly unbearable."

Boris collapsed on the bar sobbing, and now it was Horst's turn to open another bottle to try to comfort him. Boris kept on talking while sobbing and coughing:

"So, my friend, take my advice: go to Tonga... (sob, sob)... Take your time... (sob)... Learn to become as patient as they are... Learn to see the beauty in everything... Learn the innocence of a smile... Look for the good side of people... (sob, sob)... Don't look for everyone's faults to prove to yourself that you are better... (sob)... And, most of all, don't judge everything by your country's standards."

Boris was now sobbing continuously at the thought of his lost Polynesian *vahine* (Polynesian word for woman or wife). The old man had fallen into a typically Russian state of melancholy. Ten minutes later, he became silent and it was only when he started snoring that Horst realized that he was asleep.

It took Horst eight days to reach the Kingdom of Tonga; eight long days waiting for connecting flights in Auckland, Noumea, and Fiji. But in spite of the many hotels, the endless airport shuttles, the bumpy dirt roads, and the exhaustion of jet lag, Horst had found some hope in the alcoholic utterances of the old Russian. Tonga was now his promised land and he was getting closer to it every day.

Destiny can sometimes bring about the most extraordinary and unbelievable set of circumstances, as Horst found out when he arrived in the Kingdom of Tonga, a group of tiny islands on both sides of the "date line" and just below the Equator, where some ninety thousand people live precariously under the well-meaning rule of His Majesty the fat King Tupou IV, a direct descendant of a long line of Polynesian warriors.

At the airport, Horst already felt that something strange was brewing. Upon seeing his passport, the immigration officer gave him a piece of paper showing a handwritten address and politely repeated: "Repatriation, repatriation!" Through the window of the taxi driving him to the Dateline Hotel, Horst could see the few colorful streets drenched in tropical sun that make up the city of Nuku'alofa, capital of the Tonga Islands. But these were also crowded by hundreds of men with long hair and unkempt beards and women in long dresses, all of them European. Some were sitting under the huge Flamboyant trees with guitars at their side. In the town's center, he saw what looked like a tent city on the manicured lawn that stretched in front of the red-roofed Victorian-style Royal Palace. He asked the cab driver what it was all about and the embarrassing answer that he received was that these people were German "hippies." He obtained a more detailed explanation later on the hotel's patio, when he was assailed by some young folks who recognized him as a wealthy fellow citizen and invited themselves to his table:

His Majesty Tupou IV, King of Tonga, had recently been to Germany to sign a "friendship treaty," a diplomatic way of asking for financial aid in the name of his small population of fishermen and farmers. Under the impression that Tonga was a much bigger country than it was, the German government granted a sum of money way beyond the King's expectation, and in his euphoria, the overwhelmed monarch gave a long grateful speech in which he invited all German citizens to come to his kingdom where he assured they would be most welcome. His speech was broadcast on all TV channels and printed in all newspapers. Unfortunately, while His Majesty had meant tourists, many Germans, especially young hippies and "Greens" took his speech as an invitation to immigrate to his country. Soon, German pacifists, ecologists, and other counter-culture characters started dreaming of desert islands and empty beaches under swaying coconut trees ten thousand miles away from nuclear power plants, Russian missiles, and acid rain. Some rushed to sell everything they owned, from camper vans to macrobiotic tomato fields, to buy plane tickets to the Tongan Islands where a nice and chubby king was supposedly waiting for them to arrive. Entire German hippy communities thus made the long voyage to the South Pacific.

Never was his royal Majesty so taken by surprise! The small country was literally invaded by hairy, bearded, and mostly penniless crowds. In spite of the tropical heat, German-Tongan relations instantly turned icy cold. A German consular envoy was quickly dispatched from Wellington to repatriate all these "beautiful people" along with their guitars, crying babies, and marijuana seeds.

Since "German" had become a bizarre word in Tonga, Horst decided to leave this country as soon as possible. Arriving in American Samoa, Horst booked the first flight out of the Central Pacific. Destiny wanted this plane to take him to Tahiti...

During the four-hour flight, an old American lady with pink hair and bad breath sitting next to him wouldn't stop bragging about the beauty and tranquility of the island of Bora Bora.

Horst was exhausted by his long trips and emotionally drained by the successive series of disillusions. He, therefore, decided to make one last stop in that island to rest and recuperate before returning to Germany. He had abandoned his plan to find a female companion in this region.

BUT the following morning, fate had him set his suitcase in front of the reception desk of the Hotel Taina, Marcelline's small cozy world.

He spent his first twenty-four hours sleeping, enjoying the freshness of the *mara'amu*, a cool and dry wind blowing from the South and a welcome relief from the hot humidity of Manila or Pago Pago. During the first three days, the girls at the hotel didn't disturb him. During the meals, they waited on him with a smile, but in silence, and Horst spent a lot of time reading, sunbathing, and pedaling an old rusty bicycle around the island.

On the fourth day, Maïte asked him timidly how long he intended to stay at the hotel as she had to plan her reservations. By then, Horst was so happy to have found a haven of peace that he asked to stay another two weeks. He was barely recovering from the aftershock of his trip's long series of disasters and, for the first time in his life, he had no plans, no appointments, no obligations, and no deadlines. There, at the end of the world, he had found a peace of mind he had never experienced before. Slowly, however, he became aware of the surrounding little universe into which sheer luck had sent him, and he started observing the girls who ran the hotel. At first, it was with curiosity, then, little by little, with the eyes of a man not at all displeased by what he saw... All five girls were pretty, each in her own way; they all smiled a lot and were jovial, two qualities that make up half of any woman's beauty.

Knowing that he was going to stay a while at their hotel, the girls also took an increased interest in him. They started talking to him, asking him questions, and teasing him, never with disrespect, but more and more openly with less and less shyness. It turned into innocent play, which he enjoyed with much amusement. Soon, he came to realize that he couldn't wait for mealtimes and the girls' funny little routine around his table. He felt they had adopted him and he was very pleased.

At first, Maïte was his favorite, perhaps because she was more mature, more confident, and more business-like than the other girls; but he didn't show his feelings. He played the little flirting game with each one of them, something that the girls were enjoying more and more. A week after his arrival, he felt truly at home in the hotel and had adopted its pace.

On Saturday night, he decided to invite the whole play-ful quintet to go dancing at the local nightclub, a barn with a thatched roof made of coconut fronds, the dance floor facing the lagoon. The Tahitian music was blasting out of enormous speakers, but the lack of walls made it bearable while ensuring comfortable ventilation. They all had a drink at the bar, then the girls scattered through-out the room to talk to their friends among various groups of young people. In Bora Bora, everybody knows every-body. Horst sat on the side to observe the scene. The band was almost hidden by the huge pile of amplifiers and speakers. The dance floor was surrounded by benches made of coconut logs, on which young people were sitting with drinks in their hands or set on the floor in front of them.

The band started playing a *tamure* (a fast Tahitian dance) and two couples rushed to the floor to dance; the girls looked gorgeous with their bright *pareu* (a sarong-like wrap) tightly hugging their swaying hips. They danced wildly to the fast drum beat as the crowd cheered, applauded, and whistled. Horst was admiring the grace of their movements, his heart warming to the fast rhythm of the music and the whole exotic atmosphere.

A few dances later, the band began playing a slow song. Horst walked toward Maïte and invited her to dance, formally, the way they do it in Germany: he planted himself stiffly in front of her, arms parallel to his body as if at attention, then he clicked his heels and leaned forward deeply. This made quite an impression! The band stopped dead in the middle of the song and so did the dancers. Maïte was staring at him with big eyes, her hand in front of her mouth as she burst into laughter. He stood there alone feeling stupid and clumsy as the whole crowd was now laughing.

When the music started again, Horst was still standing motionless and blushing in front of Maïte. He walked with embarrassment to the bar thinking that perhaps there was some island rule forbidding the girl to dance. He stayed there a while, and drank two gin and tonics to regain countenance and courage. Since Marcelline had been sitting alone for some time, he walked toward her to invite her to dance. Again, he did his little number and, again, with the same effect: the band stopped and everybody laughed. Totally embarrassed, Horst ran out of the nightclub. He couldn't understand what had happened; after all he had been a perfect gentleman...

It was now a sad and very disappointed Horst who was walking along the road, the half moon reflected by the mirror-like lagoon guiding his steps. A motor scooter roared behind him and stopped; it was Marcelline.

"Hop on," she said. And he did, without thinking. The little two-wheeler took off and they rode in silence for about ten minutes. Horst realized the absurdity of his situation. There he was, a mature man rescued by a young girl whose long hair blowing in the wind was now caressing his face... The world was upside down...

She stopped by a beach and sat on the sand staring silently at the lagoon. Horst sat near her, keeping a respectable distance. She broke the silence to apologize for the others' behavior, and then she explained that when you want to invite a girl to dance, all you have to do is grab her hand and pull her onto the dance floor.

They stayed quiet for a long time, just looking at the silver reflection of the moon on the lagoon's ripples. Horst was watching Marcelline from the corner of his eye and it was there, in the moonlight, that he first realized that he was not with some playful teenage girl, but with a woman of exceptional beauty.

He ended up spending two months in Bora Bora. He courted Marcelline, timidly at first, then with insistence when he realized that she was not indifferent to his efforts. She saw that he seemed an honest man and she encouraged his advances with the complicity of the other girls. They became lovers a week after the nightclub fiasco and Horst fell madly in love with Marcelline. In tune with his strict German logic, he asked her to marry him and follow him to Germany. She asked to think about it for a few days, talked it over with her mother and with the other girls, and then she gave her answer:

"I'd love to come to your country, but I don't want to get married yet. Marriage is serious business, you know... But I've never been anywhere and all my friends are telling me that I should grab this opportunity to travel. So let's give it a try. But, I'm afraid to stay away from my family and my island for too long. You must promise that I can come back whenever I want."

He promised but was saddened that his marriage proposal had been turned down. As many sensitive men do, Horst suffered from much insecurity, something that was perhaps hard to explain in view of all his successful business ventures. Yet, doubts about his own value were deeply anchored in his subconscious. Also, his German-Christian ethics made him feel guilty for living out of wedlock with the young girl. He felt as if he would be cheating on her. Marrying her would have been like paying cash, and that was his way of doing business.

For Marcelline, who came from a different culture, the reasoning was different. Marriage was too serious a matter to take lightly because it involves God and is a long engagement. She liked Horst because he was kind and honest, but she wanted to try him out first, just to be sure. She felt much too young to make the big jump. Being his lover and running the risk of having his child didn't really matter. A Polynesian woman doesn't use her bed as bait or as a bargaining chip. Why should she? Both partners are equally sharing pleasure...

Marcelline lived the long flights from Tahiti to Paris in a state of panic; she remained all curled up in her seat, in a fetal position, and endured the twenty-three-hour flights like a nightmare, refusing to eat and drink on the plane.

After changing planes in Paris, they arrived in Cologne late at night. Although she was very tired when they landed, Marcelline was dazzled by the big city's millions of lights. She asked Horst:

"When do they turn off the generators?"

"Never, the lights are on all night."

"Eh, you must really like to waste electricity here!"

When the taxi dropped them off in front of Horst's apartment building, they both had to climb the stairs to the fifth floor because Marcelline refused to get locked in "that little box," the elevator. Exhausted by the climb, Horst showed her the bathroom and had to explain what a bathtub was and how to fill it up, because in the islands they only have showers. A few minutes later, he came back to see if she was all right and found her sitting in the tub in her panties and wrapped in a *pareu*.

"Why didn't you take off your clothes?"

"What kind of girl do you think I am? I don't swim naked!"

This is when Horst discovered a cultural gap he had not suspected...

The following days were spent shopping. They had to buy Marcelline a whole wardrobe of cold weather clothes. Finding shoes that would fit her feet turned out to be a major problem, as they had never been imprisoned in leather before and it was impossible to squeeze them into any kind of Western shoes. Marcelline's feet fascinated the salesman:

"This is the first time in my life I've seen feet in their natural state. What beauty!"

Finally, Marcelline left the shop wearing a large pair of size 11 AAA sneakers.

Horst was very proud of Marcelline as they walked around town. People would turn back to take a good look at her, especially impressed by her long, thick black hair. Some tried to touch it and a woman even had the audacity to pull it to see if it was real. Marcelline didn't get upset; she was just amused by the incident.

Every time they entered a large department store, the kind of place that truly amazed Marcelline, Horst noticed that, systematically, someone would leave the cash register and follow them more or less discreetly, pretending to rearrange or tag merchandise. Horst thought at first that it was to admire his exotic companion, but at the fourth department store they visited, an old lady followed them and he started having doubts. He turned around and asked:

"Why do you keep following this young lady everywhere?"

"Well, you know, it's natural, you just can't trust those gypsies! You never know!" she answered with a shrug. Horst tried to explain that Marcelline was no gypsy but a lady from Tahiti. This didn't impress the old hag. The girl looked different, foreign, and that made her suspect.

Horst felt very upset by the incident. There he was in a country where everybody dreamed of Tahiti and of her *vahines*, and when a specimen from these islands arrives as a guest, she is suspected of being a shoplifter. More unpleasant incidents, even some with his best friends, proved to Horst how difficult it was to be different within his own society. For most people, anything deviating from the regular standards of average mediocrity was looked down upon as either negative or inferior. Nobody had the time nor the desire to try to understand other cultures, to reach out to other worlds, which often have much more humane values.

The main difference between the industrialized countries and the rest of the world is perhaps that you can go to a village deep in Africa, in the Andes, or in the middle of the Pacific and when you talk, people take the time to listen and try to understand. But bring an African or a descendant of the Incas to a European town and they'll be treated with suspicion, and sometimes with hostility. Nobody will want to talk to them, let alone listen. However, if you schedule an anthropology lecture to explain these cultures and their values, people will pay to come and make a genuine effort to become interested in these societies; but getting free, spontaneous, and first-hand information was suspicious...

Fortunately, Marcelline didn't understand German and she never became aware of these contrarieties. But Horst still had to ask her to change a few of her habits, such as saying hello and smiling at everybody, because men were too quick to interpret her friendliness as an invitation.

In spite of these few vexations, Horst was now a happy man. Marcelline had redecorated his apartment with brightly colored pieces of fabric, which were now hanging everywhere, and had turned his chairs into small tables on which she displayed all sorts of shiny or colorful objects. She quickly became the neighborhood florist's best customer and gradually turned Horst's apartment into a mini-jungle of orchids, philodendrons, and other tropical plants. Every pitcher and coffee pot in the house was turned into a vase or a flowerpot. With patience, Horst let her have her way, understanding that Marcelline was missing the proximity of nature. She was just trying to recreate her familiar environment on the fifth floor of the concrete apartment building.

Marcelline was never impressed by the city's big cathedral, the high-rises, or the majestic bridges spanning the grayish Rhine River. She was, however, fascinated by the flower arrangements on the lawns in the public parks and could spend hours in deep contemplation in front of all these plants that were unknown to her.

But there were a few other things that Marcelline missed: laughing with her friends, talking to her parents, being out in the sun, and having lots of open space in which to move around and run without having to worry about breaking something. The luxurious apartment, Horst's pride, seemed like a box to her. She started getting homesick. Sometimes, at night, after looking at a photo album that she had brought along from her island, she would cry; but only when she knew Horst was asleep, for she wouldn't hurt his feelings.

Nevertheless, Horst became aware that something was wrong; Marcelline's eyes were losing their spark. He thought that she was just bored and, to keep her busy, decided to initiate her into German culture. They visited scores of castles, picturesque villages, and ancient ruins. Marcelline seemed to enjoy this frenzy of excursions and

Horst was much encouraged by her reactions. He, there-fore, decided to give a taste of great classical music to his Tahitian lady and to introduce her to the world of opera, his great personal passion.

HORST bought two tickets for the Cologne Opera for the following week when Richard Wagner's *Tannhäuser* was to be performed by the visiting cast of the Scala de Milano Opera. It was to be an exceptional evening, heralded as the highlight of Cologne's cultural season. All of the city's VIPs were to be there, even the German Prime Minister. Horst had to pay a small fortune to a scalper to obtain two front row center seats, but he didn't mind the expense as that evening at the opera was to be Marcelline's introduction to the city's high society. He wanted everybody to see her there, in the front row, facing the stage. For the first time in his life, Horst was indulging in a little showing off. He knew that all of his friends and, probably a few of his former mistresses, would be at the opera that night.

A high-fashion couturier had made a superb evening gown for Marcelline. Horst had selected a black body-fitting style with silver lamé and a high-cut Suzie Wong style slit on the side. Of course, high-heeled shoes had to be custom-made to fit Marcelline's large feet.

The big night arrived, and Horst made a much-noticed entry at the Cologne Opera. He was wearing an Italian-designed silk tuxedo with a gardenia on his lapel and fancy alligator shoes. Marcelline looked stunningly beautiful, her perfect figure emphasized by her new gown and her magnificent hair highlighted by a bright red orchid. Their arrival immediately drew a crowd. Horst's friends and business acquaintances gathered around them, waiting for their turn to be introduced to Marcelline, who was treated like a princess. They congratulated him and admitted to being somewhat envious. Horst was in utter heaven, never having been the center of so much attention. Marcelline was a little scared by her own popularity, but she held on bravely to her little purse and just kept on smiling.

The bell rang and, slowly, everybody walked into the large concert hall. The gigantic room with its huge crystal chandeliers glittering with a million sparkles and its Baroque decorations really impressed Marcelline. She even leaned over to look down into the orchestra pit where her appearance was greeted with much friendly waving from the violin section.

Horst had coached Marcelline for that evening and told her that she was about to hear the most beautiful music and the most harmonious songs in existence. Thus, it was with great impatience that he waited for her to fall under the spell.

Unfortunately, Horst didn't realize that there are two things that Tahitians can't stand: classical music in general and sopranos in particular. To them, these sounds are totally unbearable for the following reasons: the only classical music you hear in Tahiti is a little piece of Bach that is played on the radio after the day's obituaries. Therefore, any classical music is perceived as "music for the dead." Also, a soprano is a woman who screams. To a Polynesian, screaming or yelling is considered offensive, an expression of bad manners, bad taste, and rowdiness. In this context, Wagner's music wasn't the most judicious choice.

The lights dimmed, the auditorium became silent, and the orchestra started playing the overture. Wagner's heavy notes filled the room. Marcelline was surprised at first, then she grabbed Horst's arm:

"Is that your music?"

"No, no, wait! The curtain is about to rise."

The overture went on and on, somber and seemingly endless while Marcelline was getting more and more restless:

"I wanna go home, I'm *fiu* (tired, bored, fed up)!"

"Wait, wait, it's about to start!"

Indeed, the huge curtain rose and an elaborate back-drop of Black Forest scenery appeared. The great Italian diva was standing to the left, facing them. She filled her lungs and started singing an aria. Marcelline's initial marvel at the stage set-up quickly turned into irritation:

"Why is she yelling like that? Is she hurt?"

"No, no, that's the song!"

"You call that singing? I call it screaming! Can't you ask her to be quiet?"

Their conversation was received with the irritated hisses of "Shhh, shhh!" from their annoyed neighbors, big shots of Cologne high society. Horst calmly ordered Marcelline to be quiet, but she became more and more irritated. She pulled on his sleeve repeating:

"Let's go! This is awful! I wanna go home!"

"Shhh! We cannot leave now. Be patient, listen, this is beautiful."

But the more time passed, the more the fat diva screamed and the more restless Marcelline became. She had had enough of these savage yells. One last time, she begged Horst to take her home, but he kept insisting:

"Shhh, shhh, come on now... Listen, this is so beautiful."

It was simply too much. Marcelline suddenly stood up and, in a voice even louder than the fat soprano's, yelled:

"*Fiii-uuuu*!!!"

The diva choked in the middle of her aria, the conductor dropped his baton, the music stopped, and a growing murmur rose from the audience. Marcelline was now pushing her way along the first row toward the central aisle, madly kicking with her brand new pointed shoes any foot or leg that happened to be in her way. The city's notables were screaming from pain as well as outrage. A general panic developed. Nobody understood what was happening. The lights went on and the firemen on duty ran down the aisles. But an angry and determined Marcelline kept on rushing toward the exit, hitting any and everything that stood in her way, with a panicked Horst running behind her, apologizing right and left with futile attempts to explain his lady's behavior. It was in total relief that they finally reached the opera's exit.

Thus went Marcelline's much-noticed social debut in Cologne's high society. It took over half an hour for the fainted soprano to recover, to calm the audience, and to resume the performance. The next day, the incident was on the front pages of all the local newspapers.

Horst and Marcelline left for Bavaria, going into hiding for a month until everyone got over the shock of that evening. They took refuge in a small inn in the Bavarian Alps and spent their time on long mountain excursions.

Marcelline appreciated being close to nature and loved discovering the many spring flowers that were previously unknown to her. These were their happiest times together.

But after returning to Cologne, Horst renewed a very old German custom: he decided to spend every Wednesday night in his *stammtisch*. This is a table in a pub where friends meet once a week to drink and talk. Women are strictly forbidden at the meetings of this well-established custom in order to give men a brief chance to get away from the home, which is generally dominated by their wives. Horst explained this custom to Marcelline, but she didn't believe him. She couldn't understand why Horst would leave her all by herself, all night, in a foreign country, just to go talk with some friends. At first, she thought he was ashamed of her.

Being a Tahitian, she soon began to suspect that some other woman must be the reason behind Horst's weekly absences. And, of course, the more Horst insisted on going to the meetings, the more these suspicions were confirmed in Marcelline's mind. Twice she asked him to please not leave her alone at night, but Horst, used to Western women's scenes and tantrums, didn't take her sober requests seriously. He failed to understand that she was reaching the end of her rope, that she was now certain of having some female competitor, and that she had to defend herself.

The following Wednesday when Horst came home very late, Marcelline was waiting for him at the door, her body barely covered by a small *pareu*. All excited, he leaned over to kiss her, but didn't see the straight-blade razor she was holding in her hand. Her arm rose and, with one quick whack, she slashed a deep cut in his right cheek.

Blood squirted and splashed all over the furniture and the walls while Horst screamed in pain. He didn't understand, until Marcelline said coldly:

"Now, your other woman won't want you any more!"

She then burst into tears, sobbing and regretting what she had done. She got some bed sheets to stop the heavy bleeding and accompanied Horst to the hospital to get the long gaping wound sutured.

The following week, Marcelline boarded a plane to Tahiti...

Horst, now with a deep scar on his cheek, returned twice to Bora Bora. Twice he tried to talk Marcelline into coming back to Germany with him.

The first time was six months after Marcelline's return. It took Horst that long to realize how much he had gotten used to her and how much of a place she had occupied in his life. Of course, at first, he felt relieved that he no longer had to worry about Marcelline's cultural impairment. And since he had developed a taste for female companionship, he sought the company of German high-society women. But he quickly realized that these ladies' amorous embraces were leaving him totally cold. Marcelline's shadow was always looming and he was painfully missing the exotic fragrance of the *monoi* (coconut oil perfumed with Tahitian flowers) of her long hair and her body. Without that scent, other women seemed as bland as unsalted steak. But what he missed the most in those intimate moments was her spontaneity and her innocence in the sexual act. The "civilized" ladies often demanded strange, even uncomfortable positions like those pictured in erotic movies or magazines. They wanted to "fuck fashionably," as if a couple's most intimate moment was now the ultimate gadget of trendy consumerism. What an abyss between the prearranged behavior of those urban robots and the natural spontaneity, the gentleness, and the freshness of an island girl! The more Horst tried to forget Marcelline, the more painful her absence became...

THE first time Horst flew back to Bora Bora, Marcelline and her girlfriends welcomed him with great joy and with *leis* (Tahitian necklaces) made with hundreds of flowers. They lived together for a month at the hotel, pampered by the other girls. But in spite of Horst's supplications and constant begging, Marcelline refused to return to Europe. She didn't want to leave her island ever again, she said. She had had her taste of the outside world and that had been enough. Nobody smiled over there, everybody was suspicious of everybody, people were strange, and she felt so lonely, too lonely, she insisted. However, she would be glad to live with him if he decided to settle for good on Bora Bora. But Horst wasn't yet ready to exile himself on a tiny island at the end of the world.

Three years later, Horst returned to Bora Bora, this time willing to consider settling under the coconut trees. But when he stepped off the plane at the sun-drenched Bora Bora airport, he was told by the Air Tahiti agent that Marcelline was now living with a fisherman and two children in a small bamboo shack on one of the *motus* (islets) on the barrier reef that surrounds the island. Two days later, he ran into her at the Chinese general store where she arrived on an old motor scooter to buy basic supplies and kerosene for her home's lights and stove. Marcelline was thrilled to see Horst and greeted him as one would a good old friend. They set down in a snack where she brought him up to date on some of the latest island gossip and insisted that he come to visit her on her little islet. She wanted him to meet her children, her pride and joy, and to introduce him to Tihoti, her husband.

He never went...

Sweet *vahine*... sweet revenge

SOMETIMES, some of my readers complain: "Hey, your stories... don't you think they are a little too cotton candy? One sided? They often show some guy who has had all sorts of troubles, especially with European women, who shows up on your islands, finds a *vahine*, and then spends the rest of his life taking it easy under a coconut tree on the beach of some lagoon. Aren't you exaggerating a bit? Come on, admit it!"

Yes... OK, I admit that there might be some truth in these criticisms. *Vahines* (Tahitian ladies) are not all angels—far from it —and all *Popaas* (Westerners) who settle on our islands are not mentally exhausted "intellectuals" worn out by the frenetic Western civilization. To emphasize this, let me tell you the story of George:

I met George several years ago in Raiatea, an island located 50 kilometers southeast of Bora Bora. Raiatea is a fascinating place with amazing mountains and abundant wilderness. The largest of the Leeward Islands, Raiatea is an ideal agricultural island: Its vast, flat land stretches along its western shore, ready to become the breadbasket of French Polynesia. However, it is almost completely undeveloped, with the majority of the land belonging to a few landowners who seem to show more interest in land speculation than agriculture.

The capital of Raiatea is Uturoa ("big mouth" or "great power" in Tahitian, your choice). It is the administrative center of the archipelago and is home to mainly Chinese shops, government officials, French expatriates, and some *demis* (European-Tahitian mixed blood). A few years ago, Uturoa was known to be a charming little colonial town with wooden shops dating from the early 1900s. But in 1980, a major fire destroyed half of the town, after which most of the shops were rebuilt in Hong Kong style—modern concrete square boxes—without any thought for creativity or architectural harmony. Within a few years, the center of Uturoa went from a charming "fifty-years-ago Papeete" to an example of how to wipe out a very cute tropical town.

Bored expatriate government officials assigned to work in Uturoa spend most of their leisure time touring the island in their fancy cars or trying to prove their importance in one the few pubs in town. Raiatea seems to be the only Polynesian island where the rural Tahitian population tries to avoid mixing with urban people.

The lack of long, white sandy beaches—a fashionable symbol of tropical vacations—explains why the Raiatea does not interest the ordinary tourist. The only real attraction that could entice a traveler to stop in Raiatea is the great *marae* (temple) of Taputapuatea, the former sacred starting point for all great Polynesian canoe voyages. These were fantastic migrations that led the Polynesians to discover the Marquesas Islands, Hawaii (Raiatea's ancient name was "Hawaiki"), and even New Zealand.

But George wasn't interested in such historical details. The presence of a small community of expatriates in Uturoa made him decide to settle on this island. Indeed, after trying his luck in various trades without success (the story of many other drifters before him), he entered the extermination trade, hunting cockroaches, bedbugs, mosquitoes, and other insects. Most of his clients were the "white" expatriates having freshly arrived from France. These civil servants, who come at great expense to these tropical shores to accomplish a so-called "civilizing mission", cannot bear the sight of any cockroach, small lizard, mice nor mosquito, all these little creatures that thrive in our tropical moisture. Despite exquisite claims like "« Oh, what a joy to finally communicate with the beautiful Polynesian nature! » by these newcomers', their first act is to eliminate around their houses all living presence of the admired nature as quickly as possible.

It is true that it takes some time to get used to the vagaries induced by the existence in tropical latitudes. The favorite saying of an old "bushman" buddy of mine is explicit:

"The first year you live in the islands, you order a glass of draught beer at the bar. Just after it is brought to you, a big plump and shiny fly falls into the glass and starts wiggling in the foam. You call: 'Bartender, bring me another beer in another glass!'

The second year on the island, after the fly lands in your beer, you empty the glass out the window and you hold your glass out to the bartender: 'Fill her up!'

The third and fourth years, remembering the price of beer, you take your little finger and gently extract the fly struggling in the foam, you throw it on the floor and crush her with your foot, then wipe your finger on your pants and take another zip of your beer.

The fifth year, you take a long look at the fly drowning in your glass. When it finally stops moving, you think that actually it isn't quite as big as that, and you swallow it squarely with the beer.

That's when you realize that you're finally a man of the tropics."

But George and his pest-control cronies would often collect a high percentage of the expatriates' hefty paychecks, alleviating the newcomers' concerns about flies or becoming men of the tropics.

It doesn't take much to open shop as an exterminator: a pickup truck, a motorized pump with a spray nozzle at the end of a long hose, plus a dozen containers for mixing various poisons. It's obviously helpful to master a good sales pitch to be able to sell the expensive anti-termite treatment even to tenants of concrete homes, and it's equally helpful to have a catch phrase. George had chosen "Where George passes, all insects trespass!" It was painted in large black letters on his old red pickup above a huge painted centipede that ran the entire length of the vehicle. The rear gate was decorated with a hideous skull and bones.

George was excellent at his job, as if he had a personal account to settle with insects. He doubled the dose usually recommended by insecticide manufacturers; nothing survived his treatments. Sometimes the product was so strong that should an owner's cat return to the house too soon, it would also pay the price for trespassing where George has passed.

Doing things to excess was an essential trait of George's character. He boasted about past exploits more or less imaginary, and especially engaged in heavy drinking. Inevitably, he carried an enormous belly, proof of years of excessive consumption of beer and other spirits. In addition, he was a big loudmouth who thought he knew better than all others. Naturally, many people avoided him. And there are not many people on our islands.

But the cruel way he treated his wife was the reason George had earned wide disapproval among the various communities of Raiatea. Vahinatea, his *vahine*, was a simple, patient, and gentle girl who respected him. She was the epitome of the kind of woman who can still be found in remote valleys of our islands.

George had met Vahinatea seven years ago, just after he arrived on the island, in the village of Fetuna on the southern coast of Raiatea. She moved in with him after a brief courtship and encouragement by her friends and relatives, who told her:

- "Go, stay with the *Popaa*! He'll treat you well and you will have a much better life than staying here to grow food in our little patch full of stones. And then you're not going far, just a few hours' drive away."

Full of hope and her Polynesian innocence, she left her sun-baked native village one morning in George's red centipede truck, which kicked up a huge dust cloud behind. That evening she gave herself to George, her first man, as a woman gives herself to the man her heart has chosen. Since, she definitely felt like the wife of "the man who kills insects."

For the first month after their wedding, George was respectful and tender and made Vahinatea happy. But soon he started behaving again the way he had in Africa, Vanuatu, and New Caledonia. A fairly primitive man, incapable of genuine emotion, George soon got weary of Vahinatea as if he were a boy who tired of a new toy or puppy. Little by little, he began treating Vahinatea like a servant, almost a slave. Vahinatea thought his harshness was because of her pregnancy. However, the birth of their son and the return of Vahinatea's slim, girlish figure unfortunately did not change anything.

Nor did the births of their second and third children. George was just an old brute, absolutely unable to show any respect for a companion, whether African, Vanuatuan, Noumea half-cast, or Polynesian. He proved unable even to provide his family with decent material comfort, not because he didn't earn a good living but because he squandered much of his income on drinking and boasting in bars, looking for some new lost soul to impress. Inevitably, when he came home drunk at night—which was very common—he would be in a bad mood and would beat his wife, even his children when they were frightened and would begin to cry.

Vahinatea, a true Polynesian and deeply religious woman, took the beatings and accepted her fate. To her, George was her companion and the father of her children. She had to stay with him; if he was mean, that meant that she simply had had bad luck. Her education commanded her to stay with him, at his side, and the blows she received made no difference.

The only time she really hated George, when she could even have killed him, was when he insulted her in public and called her vile names. He even once slapped her in front of other people. In these painful moments, he touched her dignity, her last refuge, so important to the Polynesians whose standing in the community is of vital importance. Afterwards, she dared not go out anymore, holing up at home for years like a wounded animal. She did not want to suffer the shame of being seen with George, who had lost all credibility and all respect from the native population.

George also was one of those people who believe they are superior, eternal beings and think that misfortunes only befall others. Thus, in his work, he neglected the most elementary safety rules. He worked shirtless and breathed without a mask, not worrying about effects of chemicals like dioxin and other carcinogens he was using every day with his customary generosity. Several customers had remarked about this, but he only replied laughing: "These gadgets are for tenderfeet!"

Inevitably, George began to cough one day. The cough worsened over time. The emergence of a chronic illness didn't prevent the bully from continuing to drink—quite the contrary. Quickly, George's coughing became a familiar sound in the bars along the main street of Uturoa. Its frequency and severity grew stronger.

Then it suddenly stopped. George did not come to the bars anymore.

Nobody saw him for months. The unusual quietness in the bars of Uturoa raised some eyebrows. Some of the old-time expatriates didn't really become concerned, but were curious. Thus I was picked to go to George's house to discover the reason for his prolonged absence.

I DROVE they Jeep up the rough dirt road in the valley of Tevaitoa. George's boxy plywood house of a common Polynesia type soon appeared on the right. The courtyard was clean and full of flowers, and the house had even been recently repainted. Laundry was drying on a wire stretched between an avocado tree and a coconut tree. It was obvious that a traditional *vahine* occupied this plot of land and managed to give it a look of happiness and cleanliness, despite the limited material means available. George's pickup with its gigantic centipede was parked next to the house with one flat tire. The vegetation around the edge of the pickup indicated that it had not been moved for quite some time.

Vahinatea sat on the door steps, peeling cassava tubers. Her long hair was divided into two braids and she was wearing a blue *pareu* (sarong) that suited her very well. She was alone; the children were at school. I parked the Jeep in front of the house and greeted her. She replied with a smile and raised her head for the usual kissing.

- "Hello, Vahinatea. Everything alright?" I asked.
- "*E. Maitai roa!*" ("Great!")
- "And George? Is he at home?"

Her face darkened.

- "Yes, in the back," she mumbled.
- "Can I see him?"
- "If you insist..."

She rose abruptly and preceded me into the house. We crossed the small room.

The house was clean, and the sun shone between the curtains of the flowery fabric hung in the windows. Cushions embroidered with colorful *tifaifai* patterns, so typical of Polynesian houses, were well highlighted on beds and chairs. Everything appeared cheerful and happy... until she opened a door at the end of the short hallway.

Never shall I forget what followed:

A foul stench escaped the tiny room and hit me. Then I saw the horrible spectacle and I wanted to vomit. George—or, rather, what appeared to be George—was lying on a bed stained with the blood that was trickling out of his mouth. It had covered his chest, saturated his dripping sheets, and even formed puddles on the floor. That blood was black, partly dried, and cracked in places,

121

like if it was some kind of tar. Frightened by my arrival, thousands of enormous green flies suddenly exploded from the puddles of blood and began to hum in the air around me, hitting my face, obscuring the light of the room. I tried to struggle against this terrible cloud, but it was to no avail.

Thin to the bones and appearing twenty years older, it seemed George was dying of some lung disease. The black, viscous fluid kept flowing from between his lips. He slowly turned his head and looked my way through the swarm of flies. His eyes were wide open and expressed sheer terror, a look that made me shiver. He tried to speak. Only a gasp, a gurgle was audible. Instead of words, more black blood jelly bubbled out of his mouth. I held my hand over my nose, trying to block the terrible stench, repressing my urge to throw up. I was petrified by the supreme horror around me.

But then my feelings of sickness and terror quickly turned to anger:

- "Why haven't you cleaned him up?" I asked Vahinatea, who had remained passive in the hallway. "What are you waiting for? How can you...?"

- "Oh... So you want me clean him?" she said dryly. "Okay, I'll do it."

She ran out of the house but immediately returned with a garden hose. Then she started to hose down everything: the sick man, the walls, the filthy bed. She flooded everything with the nozzle wide open. She directed the jet of water straight at George without worrying if he would choke or drown. A stinking mixture of clotted blood, dead flies, and water began to trickle down the hallway. But Vahinatea continued to point the hose right onto the bed with her icy stare. George tried to move but was too weak, and could not cough because of the black liquid.

I just couldn't stand watching this horrible spectacle any longer and started to go outside to vomit, but Vahinatea held me firmly back by the hand. That is when she told someone for the first time what had been in her heart for so long:

- "Just stay here and look! Watch how I treat the monster that beats his own children! Watch how I treat the husband who prefers to drink rather than take care of his family! Watch how I treat the man who humiliates me, who ruined my youth. This is what the man who made me cry every night and every day for years deserves!

"Let him die quickly. I am at peace. I know that the Lord understands me!"

She slammed the door of the dying man's room, then flushed the corridor clean and neatly rolled up the garden hose outside while I hurried back to my Jeep.

Two days later, at the Uturoa hospital, George fell into a coma and quickly died of lung cancer. Because Vahinatea was a member of the Adventist Church, the little religious community rushed to take care of the funeral and collect money for her and her children. It is also thanks to that religious community that some people were present to attend George's burial.

The evening after the funeral, all the regulars of he Uturoa bars were very silent. None of them had attended the funeral of the man who for years had tried so hard to impress them.

Maybe there are more Vahinateas and Georges in our islands than one might have thought...

"Tropical High Society"

MANY years ago, when I travelled to 'civilized' countries, people would ask me the same question: "How can you live down there on those lost islands where it is so difficult to find the things necessary to lead a civilized life?"

Of course, not too long ago when supermarkets and other large stores did not yet exist in Tahiti, we did not have the same selection of goods as one had in Paris or Los Angeles. Far from it! Often we had to wait six months to find an out-of-the-ordinary object that we wished to buy. At that time, the rule of thumb in Tahiti was that if you saw something special for sale, you had to buy it right away—at a tremendous price of course—

because there would be none left the following day. Thus, we quickly learned to be satisfied with the strictly necessary, just as we had to learn patience.

But having so few goods available does not mean that our islands lacked class. Quite the contrary, sometimes they even have more class than continental cities; but differently, of course. This class was—and still is—very unique to the Islands, a class that I discovered long ago in Tahiti, at the residence of Maïre F. Let me recount this memorable experience:

Maïre was a beautiful woman who wore her thirty years well. Slim, of medium height, she moved about with an elegance that our girls acquire thanks to extended training sessions with one of the numerous Tahitian dance groups, which actually act as some sort of finishing school for our young girls. Of course, Maïre, like any self-respecting real Tahitian, had her long, long black hair floating in the wind, hair that had a tendency to slide forward and cover part of the face. This obstruction of the face was taken care of with a sudden strong movement of the head that would throw the long hair to the back where it belonged, creating long undulations throughout the hair. I love this gesture, so typical of our islands girls. All of Polynesia does this gesture.

Maïre's mother was a pure Polynesian from Rurutu, one of the Austral Islands. Her father, an Englishman who arrived in the 1930s, had introduced beekeeping to Tahiti. Thus Maïre was a *Demie* (half-cast)—as it's said in Tahiti without any pejorative implication—who had inherited her father's Western ambition, while her mother had passed on her Polynesian patience, kindness, and calm. But it is a calm that covers pure Maori pride, very sensitive to contrarieties, like a dormant volcano waiting under a lava field. So when our Tahitian girls are really upset, a major eruption may occur. When this happens, it's better to leave, hide, and wait for the storm to pass. Most important, one must not try to convince or calm such raging fury, or it will only get worse.

When Maïre celebrated her eighteenth birthday, her father took her on a long journey in order to present her to the European branch of his family in England; a journey of discovery that branded our Maïre forever. Over there in Europe, she discovered what some call the finer things in life: elegant receptions, formal dinners, balls with their waltzes, tea ceremonies; in brief, all the social ceremonial trappings known as civilization in the United Kingdom. Maïre's aunt, who was a 'dynamo' of the local "gentry" of London, explained at length and in detail the many secrets of proper etiquette; the right moves to be made at the right time by a person of quality and worthy of her social rank. This training included the art of choosing the proper objects to furnish and decorate a home, and how to dress for a particular occasion. Thus, little by little, with patience and much effort, the old aunt infused into Maïre something that was quite unknown to the Polynesians: class consciousness.

Young Maïre was the best student her aunt could have possible found. She did absorb with enthusiasm and great ease all the ceremonial rites of the English gentry, which was logical because the foundation of Polynesian society is also based on a complicated system of rituals, though quite different. Two centuries ago, Omai, the first Tahitian to visit London, had enthused English royalty thanks to the apparent civility in his gestures and his extraordinary adaptation to a society that gave exaggerated importance to ceremonials. Thus, he superbly confirmed—without knowing it—the theory of the "noble savage," announced a few decades earlier in the writings of Jean-Jacques Rousseau.

After her year-long educational trip to Europe, Maïre returned to Tahiti with a firm and precise goal: she would become the social *"grande dame"* of Papeete, Tahiti's capital. Such a sophisticated way of life had now become her obsession. She quickly abandoned her boyfriend, who did not conform to her new ambitions anymore, to look for a husband who had the financial means to provide for an English lady living in style at the antipodes. Thus, Maïre began to frequent the government circles and accepted all invitations to be able to review all available bachelors, especially the *Popa'a*, the Western foreigners.

Of course, being intelligent she carefully hid her true ambitions because she knew very well that the reason why many *Popaas* marry Tahitian women is precisely to escape the ordeal and expenses tied to the social ambitions of some of the Western ladies. Only after the wedding would she, little by little, reveal her secret goal, with kindness and infinite patience. One thing that our island girls are good at is taking control of their husbands, especially *Popaa* husbands; but they always do so intelligently, with sensitivity, and with great respect for the dignity of the husband: they make him believe he actually is in charge.

Maïre found a suitable husband in the person of Jean-Marc, a high ranking civil servant who had been transferred to Tahiti many years ago. He was forty years old, divorced, still handsome, and virile. His salary guaranteed a comfortable life and security, his high position ensured a respected place in the small social circles of Papeete. The way to access all the beautiful things that seem to be essential for a certain conception of quality of life was thus found.

In return, Maïre brought Jean-Marc delightful company, reliable contact with the local population, and she ensured that he would remain based in Tahiti (with all the privileges that this entailed) because the French government, sensitive to local circumstances, considered it cruel to ask a Tahitian to live in the coolness of the distant motherland.

After a discreet marriage, Maïre went on to work on her dream. She chose a large plot of land in the heights of Punaauia, today the chic suburb of Papeete, and a few years later, had a large house built on it. It was of Victorian style with a wide terrace on one side. The choice of location was perfect because it offered a superb view over the Sea of the Moon, the stretch of ocean between Tahiti and Moorea; the peaks of the island of Moorea as the backdrop resembled Chinese shadows at sunset.

It took Maïre nearly ten years before she was satisfied with her acquisition of all the essential objects needed to be a *grande dame*. She planted herself a beautiful garden, getting shoots of rare plants from old Harrison-Smith at his property in Papeari. Because crystal glasses, Wedgewood china, or Christofle silverware were, at the time, either unknown in Tahiti or horribly expensive, getting the right china and silverware was her most difficult and time-consuming chore. To work around this dilemma, she renewed a friendship with an old schoolmate from the Pomare High School, who had since become a stewardess for UTA Airlines. She persuaded her friend to bring on each trip a few crystal glasses, a few dishes, a few silver spoons; items purchased according to Maïre's precise directions in Paris or Los Angeles and smuggled into Tahiti—and this lasted for years. One really has to admire how much energy, patience, and love Maïre invested in creating her small, refined abode on an island at the end of the world.

And with time, her home in Punaauia became a temple of Western civilization and refinement but with a definite Tahitian touch, this in a society that was still very isolated and rural.

During one of my visits to Tahiti in 1979, I had the honor of receiving an invitation to have dinner at Maïre and Jean-Marc's home. Someone had certainly exaggerated my social rank or my intellectual capacities to the extent that the couple considered me worthy of such an invitation. Indeed, Jean-Marc drove himself to pick me up at the hotel. I was very flattered by this honor, as the reputation of the quality of their hospitality and the beauty of their home had already crossed the oceans. In Suva, Fiji, I had heard a diplomat rave about Jean-Marc and Maïre's lifestyle.

The house turned out to be even more beautiful than I had thought possible. I have always been in love with this tropical colonial style, called "Victorian" in former British colonies, "Gingerbread" in the USA, and "Pomare" or "*fare vanira*" (vanilla house) in French Polynesia. These large houses are painted all in white and have no windows; only doors that are left open and adorned with colorful printed cotton curtains, allowing the cool air on the ground to enter the house and provide a natural freshness much more pleasant than air conditioning. These houses are almost always completely surrounded by covered verandas with intricately carved braces at the corner posts. After having experienced the pleasant and natural freshness of these houses, which are so well adapted to the tropical climate, the current fashion of housing people in air-conditioned concrete boxes seems incongruous, even absurd .

Maïre was waiting for us on the terrace at the top of the stairs. She was really a most beautiful woman. Proud but not snobbish, her long black hair accented by the contrast of a long, white embroidered gown, she seemed to be in perfect symbiosis with the house and the surrounding lush tropical garden. The whiteness of her dress only gave more warmth to the smoothness of her copper-colored skin, her slightly almond-shaped eyes adding just the right touch of exoticism. So much beauty, grace, refinement in fairy tale surroundings awakened in me old

131

childhood dreams, romantic and impossible: Maïre seemed to be a tropical Snow White princess. My admiration could be read on my face, and Jean-Marc beamed with pride. He introduced us. In Tahitian fashion, she used the familiar French "*tu*" right away, which pleased me a lot because it showed not only a respect for the customs of Tahiti, but also made me immediately feel as if I was being accepted as an intimate by this beautiful tropical Eve. I complimented her on her home, which she accepted with humility and retired to leave us men alone.

A Tahitian girl draped in a *pareu* (sarong) served us drinks on the terrace. Everything was just perfect. In front of us, the sun setting behind the island of Moorea began its magic show; the majestic peaks of the island, with little clouds clinging to their summits, appeared to be volcanoes spewing smoke. The ballet of the sunset's successive reds set the horizon ablaze. The gin and tonics were great, and the conversation interesting. Jean-Marc turned out to be an expert in Pacific history and an inexhaustible source of anecdotes about the vicissitudes of life on the islands. Time passed too quickly, and soon it was time to move to the dining table.

And what a grand table it was! Worthy of the Elysée or Buckingham Palace. The tablecloth was of the finest embroidered linen. The stemware had the slight bluish reflection that betrays true crystal. The decanters on the table revealed the velvety colors of excellent wine, certainly chosen with care. Facing each plate was a small vase holding an anthurium, a floral decoration that was complemented by a large arrangement of birds of para-

dise at the end of the table. The furniture was of mahogany in the Louis-Philippe style, with chairs covered
with blue silk brocade. Paintings and black and white
photographs of family ancestors, framed with gold,
adorned the white walls. A huge ceiling fan with wooden
blades turned slowly to help circulate the cool air entering from the terrace. Along the doors, Tahitian style flow-
ered cotton curtains swayed to the rhythm of the breeze.
It was with astonishment that I realized how much their
marriage with classical European furniture can be a real
success.

All this was so astounding, so beautiful, and so refined
that I remained speechless. During my many travels,
nowhere in the world had I ever seen so much good taste
in such idyllic surroundings—a real dream. At last, I had
found the essence of the mirage that attracts so many
Westerners to the tropical Pacific islands. I felt jealous
of Jean-Marc, of his success, of his wife, and of him for
having such a perfect life style.

We took our places at the table. Across the table sat an
old, proud Polynesian lady with a wrinkled face, long
braided white hair hanging in her back. She nodded her
head my way with a big smile; her way to say hello. Jean-
Marc introduced her as Maïre's mother, and explained
that she only spoke the Rurutu dialect and Tahitian. At
the end of the table, to the left of this lady, sat a boy and
a girl, both about ten years old. They were introduced as
the twins, the children of Maïre and Jean Marc. They also
gratified me with a big smile and a certain shyness.

The girl dressed in the *pare'u* brought the appetizers,
shrimp cocktails. Jean-Marc served wine and the con-

versation resumed. I again complimented my hostess on the quality of her hospitality, and the conversation turned to the problems related to the isolation of French Polynesia from the rest of the English-speaking South Pacific islands. Jean-Marc explained that this isolation was due to a new virus that proliferates in Tahiti since the start of the 1960s, the *"bacterium neuroticum anglophobia."* We were all laughing at the joke when a young lady made her entrance on the terrace. Just as beautiful and elegant as Maïre, she was introduced as Tiare, her younger sister.

She bestowed a quick smile upon us all, then stood beside the table and whispered to Maïre. The girl with the *pareu* brought the next course, a huge and beautifully cooked lagoon parrot fish covered with some fancy seasoned mayonnaise. Tiare refused the invitation to join us for dinner and then began to have a louder argument with Maïre. She was asking why Maïre had killed her dog. Maïre calmly explained that it had been an accident, that the poor dog had been lying under her car where she could not see him. Tiare wasn't satisfied with the answer. Gradually, the argument between the two sisters became more tense, and the vocabulary quickly became much less distinguished.

Soon, a real scene developed between the women, and they both started screaming at each other, first in French then in Tahitian. I could not understand what was being yelled, which was certainly better for my chaste ears. The yelling between the two women became increasingly louder and faster when, suddenly, I saw the mother and the children quickly dive under the table. Wondering why, I turned my head toward the arguing women: I saw a furious Tiare step slowly toward the table, firmly grab the tablecloth with the long fingernails of both hands, take a step back and—tchac—pull hard. That's when everything flew across the room—the fish, the cut crystal decanters, the Wedgewood china, the flowers and vases, the rice pilaf, the superb glasses. Everything became airborne! Strangely, the silverware seemed to fly faster than the rest. And everything went crashing against the wall to my left in a huge roar, creating a sinister mix of linen, crystal, wine, broken china, mayonnaise, and other food.

In an instant, the beautiful terrace, the symbol of supreme refinement in the tropics, had been transformed into a battle zone.

The wine, like blood, was now dripping from the ancestors' portraits. The beautiful flowers were bathing in a pool of red wine under an overturned chair. A piece of the beautiful fish, stuck to the wall by the spicy mayonnaise, was slowly sliding toward the floor, leaving a yellow trail on the white wall.

The sister disappeared after shouting a last Maori warrior scream, shaking the house while running on the balcony.

Slowly, the old lady and the children, impassive as if they were familiar with such a cyclone, reappeared from under the table. Jean-Marc and I remained motionless, covered with sauce, rice and wine, both still stunned by the disaster that had unfolded before our eyes.

That's when Maïre stood up, threw her long hair back with a head movement—which made a little more rice fly in my direction—and while using a towel to try to clean her dress which had become very colorful, gave me a big smile and said:

"As you can see, we Tahitians, we have a lot of character. Come, let's have coffee on the terrace!"

Now that's what I call "true class".

The Mystery of the Vaiami Hospital

IN THE Western section of Papeete, the small capital of the island of Tahiti, there is still an island of peace dating back to colonial times. This place is the Vaiami Hospital, formerly called Colonial Hospital, the last surviving buildings of a neighborhood built in the 1880s; a splendid example of the military architecture of the French Second Empire.

Single-floored, rectangular buildings surround a small park with a huge palm tree in the center. The roofs are covered with red shingle imported from France in the 19th century, carried as ballast onboard military sailing ships to allow them to better sail against the head winds around Cape Horn. These tiles cover large protruding roofs whose riveted cast iron rafters rest on elegant

137

wrought iron columns. Under these roofs, beautiful cast iron balustrades and benches form the open-air corridors that allow one to walk in the shade from room to room or to the neighboring buildings.

This hospital looks like a sister to other such establishments that one can find in cities such as Pondicherry, Dakar, or Cayenne, all former cornerstones of a glorious French colonial past. The military architects of Napoleon III had managed to create a style that was admirably well adapted to the heat, humidity, and the slow pace of tropical life.

Not so long ago, the entire neighborhood surrounding the hospital consisted of many such solid century-old buildings. But suddenly, like a cyclone, the fashion of modernism and a passion for air-conditioned concrete boxes spread to Tahiti. It erased all memories of past ways of living more effectively than a horde of barbarians could have done, so that today, the survival of the Vaiami complex seems more due to a miracle than an act of reason.

Some 40 years ago, a new large and more modern hospital made its appearance on the other side of the town of Papeete. All health services hurried there, attracted by the new and shiny. The old hospital then remained abandoned; used to store archives, forgotten like a toy in which a spoiled child has lost all interest.

Yet, the newly introduced modern lifestyle severely affected the fundamental values of the fragile Polynesian society of the small tropical island of Tahiti. Like some proof of the supposedly "successful" modernization of society, a growing number of mental cases quickly developed within the urban population. Thus, the Vaiami Hospital rapidly found itself a new vocation; it was turned into the psychiatric center of French Polynesia— in other words, the lunatic asylum.

ONE cool July morning, in this protected medical center, began a medical case that will certainly leave its mark in the annals of world psychiatry.

That day, as doctors and psychiatrists held their usual morning conference and discussed cases in treatment, a young Tahitian man who appeared to be about twenty-five years old, appeared before them, a large bundle in his hand. He was a tall, handsome man who proudly wore the athletic build of the Polynesians. Barefoot, he was dressed in cotton shorts and a blue T-shirt. His rough, strong hands betrayed a history of manual work. His eyes were jet black and pleated because he constantly smiled gently, almost softly. He seemed pleased and satisfied to be before all these medical personnel. In Tahitian fashion, he walked around the table, shaking hands with every one of the surprised doctors.

The doctors questioned him, but he answered in Tahitian. They called a nurse-translator.

"I'm here to stay. My name is Timi."

And he started again to walk around the table and to again shake hands with everyone; doctors and nurses. He seemed happy. He looked around the room, examined every painting and poster on the walls, and every piece of furniture, letting his hand glide over the white lacquered cabinets that stood along one of the walls.

The psychiatrists were surprised, but kept their cool. Patience is of the essence in the world of psychiatry. They questioned him for the next two hours, but could only understand that his name was Timi and that he had come to stay at the Vaiami Hospital. And from what he had been able to observe so far, it seemed to suit him perfectly. It was impossible for the doctors to obtain more information, even essential details such as his family name and his usual place of residence. He said only that he had come from the islands. The nurse-translator thought she recognized the Leeward Islands' way of talking, the one that was used on the islands of Huahine, Raiatea, and Bora Bora.

At last, the doctors had to explain to Timi that it was impossible for him to stay. That Vaiami was a hospital, not a hotel. The young man looked astonished, and repeated:

"But my name is Timi. I've come to stay. I have to stay here."

Lengthy explanations lasted the rest of the day. Nothing could sway the determination of the young man. And in the evening, he was expelled from the hospital, yet gently and without force.

Despite the eviction, Timi did not lose his smile. Quietly, he unrolled his bundle, spread his *peue* (woven pandanus mat) under the roof of the ancient gate next to the gatekeeper's house, and settled for the night.

Doctors also know how to be stubborn. For two days they left him sitting in front of the gate. Yet, Timi did not budge. He talked to passersby who wanted to talk, and ate sandwiches that other Tahitians offered him. He had befriended one of the guards and talked freely with him. He never entered the hospital except to use the bathroom.

The third day, astonished by such insistence, the psychiatrists questioned the guard to try to garner more information. He explained what he had learned:

"This young man is from some farm. His father, whom Timi highly regards, just died. We mainly talked agriculture. He is a specialist in bananas, *tarua*, and pumpkins. He is also a very polite person; he has no meanness. He has had a good education. He is a Christian and seems to have attended Sunday school as he often quotes Bible verses in good Tahitian. He seems to have done little or no regular schooling. This is his first trip to Tahiti. He does not know anyone here. But he says he must stay in the hospital. He said the hospital, this hospital here, is his home. So he stays."

For humanitarian reasons, and because he was embarrassed by the spectacle of this man sleeping on his porch, the chief medic decided to house him in one of the cells of the hospital pending the outcome of the investigation to be carried out by the police, who had just been notified of the case.

Timi settled in his cell, smiling even more happily now. He walked around the hospital, and shook hands with all the patients and employees. He even offered to help with the work.

A Tahitian police inspector arrived the following morning. Four hours of intensive questioning did not unveil any additional information. This nice, well-mannered young man was a total enigma. He seemed to have arrived from nowhere. He merely repeated: "I must stay here, it's my home."

Before leaving, the police officer took his fingerprints and his photograph so that they could be broadcast on television news and in the local newspapers. Alas, a few days later, not one person had called; no one had recognized him. Nobody appeared to know Timi. This was strange; even more so in Tahiti, which was such a small country.

Two weeks later, the police returned, still empty-handed. None of the investigations, even in the outer islands, had resulted in even the slightest lead. But they had formulated a plan, which they explained to the psychoanalysts:

"We'll forcibly put him on the Leeward Islands schooner. We have bought him a ticket all the way to Bora Bora. When he arrives, he will recognize it and disembark to return home. The supercargo will tell us the name of that island and we will continue our inquiries from there. The schooner *Temehani* sails tomorrow night. We'll pick him up one hour before sailing time."

They came to get him. They put him on the boat.

Yet four days later, Timi was back, smiling, sitting on his bed, though with a nice tan gotten during his small island cruise.

This time, it was the captain of the police force who came to bring some news:

"When he boarded the island schooner, he asked the supercargo where they were sailing. The latter explained to him that the boat was calling at every island all the way to Bora Bora, as well as on the return voyage. Yet, Timi never stepped off the boat. He talked with many Tahitian passengers, although he did not seem to know any of them. The supercargo wanted to let him off the schooner in Bora Bora as he had neither a return ticket nor money, but Timi refused. Upon his return to Papeete, he even complimented the captain for the quality of the food onboard his ship. The shipping company handed us the bill to pay for his return passage and his meals.

"We asked all the police stations on the Leeward Islands to investigate. We sent his fingerprints to the central national file. Nothing! He just isn't known anywhere. He has not even done his mandatory military service. He seems to have completely bypassed the bureaucratic system until now. He appears to have dropped out of nowhere. A truly exceptional case... He is yours!"

"Oh, no," replied the chief doctor, "we can't keep him. He does not appear mentally disturbed. He even seems very normal. He is your responsibility now. Keep him."

"But what do you want me to do?" asked the police officer. "He has committed no crime. He is not on any wanted list; quite the contrary, as he appears not to exist officially. Simply show him the door."

"We tried. He just won't leave. He seems fascinated by this hospital. It's a mystery."

The police officer thought for a long time while rubbing his chin; then decided:

"Okay. I'll hold him in jail for seventy-two hours for vagrancy, as permitted by law. But I'll have to release him then. Perhaps he'll understand the lesson and will then return home, wherever that is."

The police officer left the hospital holding Timi with one hand and carrying the bundle with the other.

But two days later, in the morning when the medical team arrived, Timi was again sitting on his bed, smiling. The chief doctor called the police for an explanation. The police officer arrived an hour later, very nervous:

"He escaped. As he is not aggressive at all, in fact, he's very helpful, we had him assigned to help out in the prison kitchen. He apparently escaped by hiding in the garbage dumpster. Please do not tell this to anyone, or we will have to bear another media campaign making fun of us, calling our prison a sieve. It's good that he is back here, because now he is yours."

"Oh no, you take him back to prison!" demanded the chief doctor.

"Listen, doctor. Be lucid. A man escapes from prison to return to the nuthouse, which, in fact is just another prison. If you are looking for an abnormal being, well here you got one superb sample. I'll write a document to that effect."

"We're not a nuthouse, officer! We are a psychiatric hospital. We heal people, we do not incarcerate them!"

"Call it what you wish, Doctor. But Timi seems not to have his head on quite right. So, treat him well, since it is your job and your passion. He's all yours. Goodbye, gentlemen."

And the police officer disappeared, too happy to have closed another case.

The following day's doctors' conference was entirely devoted to the Timi case. Now that the young man's presence in the hospital was backed by some legal document, some psychiatrists were actually quite happy. Before them was an exceptional case indeed. Because of his peaceful and pleasant personality, Timi only made the case more interesting. For a change, they did not have the usual symptoms of schizophrenia, which was common among some *demis,* the mixed-blood population of Tahiti that often feels torn between two cultures. Nor was this a case of depression or violence resulting from frustration caused by a new world of material values. Surprisingly, the psychiatrists were actually competing to treat Timi, and the chief doctor had to make a choice. He entrusted Timi's case to Dr. Gomez.

Dr. Julie Gomez seemed to be a good choice. A woman in her late forties, tall, thin, and still very beautiful, Julie was the most experienced psychoanalyst of the group. For almost fifteen years, she had worked as assistant to the famous professor Jean Sonnblum at the La Salpetrière Hospital in Paris. Dr. Julie Gomez was recognized as an authority on mood disorders and obsessive compulsive disorders, specializing in phobic disorders. The obsession from which Timi suffered seemed to fit into that category.

The presence of a specialist of this caliber in a small unit like the Vaiami Hospital, lost at the bottom of the world, was astonishing: a widow after the accidental death of her husband, and mother to two adult children who had achieved their own professional success, Dr. Julie Gomez decided to exile herself to discover a different environment. She hoped that new horizons would help to fill the void left by her late husband.

She never regretted her choice of Tahiti. She discovered with amazement a society undergoing a profound change, a community that was just beginning to produce the first symptoms of "civilized" mental disorder. It was with fascination that she observed a population for whom until now the word "future" had little meaning, nor had it been the subject of any concern before, take an eager dive into the traps of a consumer economy. It would later find itself trapped by the constraints and loss of freedom that "easy credit" and the lust for material possessions bring.

Perceiving more clearly than any other observer the fatal slope down which the small community of Tahiti was sliding, she would have liked to scream warnings from her experience before it was too late, before the islanders would lose their unique nonchalance and their smiles. Several times she had spoken about her concerns to the head doctor, but he advised her not to make any announcements:

"We are a small team of psychiatrists, not sociologists. We are here to heal, not to change society. And, most importantly, criticizing the system being introduced will be perceived by local politicians as a personal attack against their efforts toward 'modernization.' Come, my dear Julie, you know as well as I that these gentlemen feel so insecure about themselves that they need all these very expensive shiny gadgets so they can prove their importance to themselves each day. Didn't you tell me yourself that the big SUVs with chrome accessories have become the pacifier that calms a whole social class of Tahiti? So let's not make waves; let's just do our job. That way we also ensure that they'll need our services in the future, no?" he concluded with a sly smile.

With ardor and passion, Julie immersed himself in Timi's case. The softness of the young man's personality was intriguing and touching at the same time. To some

145

degree, maternal instinct certainly influenced the intensity of her interest. Assisted by Augustine, the oldest nurse-interpreter, she began by making Timi follow the full range of standard psychological tests. She then spent entire weeks questioning him to make him talk so that she could explore the recesses of his brain and, more essentially, gain his trust.

She went from surprise to surprise. Before her stood an individual who was totally at ease, fully confident in himself, with a solid base; but this base seemed fundamentally shaken. His reflexes and reactions seemed not to be dictated either by sequels of youth trauma, the desire to want to impress, nor by a search for affection or recognition. Timi stood in stark contrast to modern man whose behavior is generally motivated either by ambition, a competitive spirit, or a quest for security.

This created quite a few problems for Julie. First, a psychiatrist must be able to fit a patient into a specific category. Yet, with Timi, the category into which he would fit just didn't seem to exist. The second problem was that a psychiatrist must put his patient into a state of vulnerability, of dependency or anxiety, in order to be able to create a therapy relationship. This was not happening with Timi. Also, in order to detect mental problems, it is imperative to find the key element that motivates the existence of any individual; that 'little bug' that 'ticks' in the heart or the soul of a person. And this pulse is usually deeply hidden in the dark recesses of the subconscious.

But the inner world of Timi appeared to be a simple and solid universe, controlled by a healthy logic of reasoning; yet, sometimes quite oriental. Symbols were the predominant elements of his scale of values; especially biblical symbols such as God and the devil. All his words were coherent, well structured, and very important to him, which is quite logical for someone who could neither read nor write. When Timi announced that he would do something, he would do it thoroughly, even if the task required superhuman effort. He had a total respect for the given word.

He also had a great sense of community living that seemed innate. He shared everything with others, something that some of the other patients abused constantly. If you spoke to him at mealtimes, he would automatically offer you the food on his plate, and you had to eat at least one piece so as not to offend him. Julie was betting everything on this community spirit to try to access the key to the mystery. She questioned him continuously about the community that he had left behind, and on the reason behind his departure. But his answer was always the same:

"It does not matter why I left. It is the past, so it has ended. My father told me that here is my real family. That's why I'm here. A son must obey his father, so say the Scriptures."

Then he would show a big smile in order to avoid delving further into the subject. Julie imagined then a father, seeing his son develop some mental problem, giving the order to go to the psychiatric hospital in Papeete and to stay there. But she could not detect any apparent mental disorder in this young man, apart from this unshakable stubbornness in wanting to stay at the Vaiami Hospital. Why would a father want his son to spend his life in a mental asylum? No, the key must be elsewhere. She had to find it.

A year later, Julie still wasn't any closer to solving the riddle. But she had learned to deeply appreciate the human being in Timi. He was a righteous man, a being whom you could trust absolutely. Seeing him always smiling, cheerful, and quick-witted, she counted the

Alex W. du PREL

numberless hours spent in consultation with him among
the pleasant moments of her days.

In the first few months, he had, of course, repeatedly
tried to seduce her. But she pushed him away gently, and
eventually he no longer insisted. Julie was actually quite
flattered by the advances made, but understood that this
was a compliment to her femininity, as well a gesture
from Timi to show her that he was a man complete and
normal. She even felt a little guilty one evening after one
of these advances, when she surprised herself by spending almost an hour primping and preening in front of her
mirror.

Timi had created his niche in the small world of the Vaiami Hospital. Despite protests from doctors, he had
gradually assumed the position of house painter. He
proved to be extremely meticulous in his work, and any
speck of dirty or peeling paint was immediately cleaned
and covered with a new layer.

The spectacle of Timi strolling about the grounds with
pot and brush had become a daily routine. He pampered
the buildings and everyone had to admit that the maintenance had never been so conscientiously executed.

He also quickly learned some rudimentary French and
was improving day by day, so much so that now Julie
could do without an interpreter during their everyday
consultations. He was most curious and wanted to know
everything. Thus, following the daily morning visit by
the group of doctors, the other internees also became ac-
customed to receiving Timi as a visitor. Wearing his big
smile, Timi would pop into the room and question them,
and make wholesome small talk. Soon, Timi acquired the
nickname *taote Tahiti* (Tahitian doctor), and he was most
popular with all employees and patients. (It should be explained here that hospitals in Tahiti are much more open

and allow freer access than those in other countries. There is constant traffic of family members visiting their sick because no Polynesian would leave a parent alone in a hospital; it would be like abandoning him. The islands' dispensaries even provide beds for family members during childbirth stays.)

But let's return to Timi. After the young man had spent two years at the Vaiami Hospital, doctors held a meeting to review his case. They questioned Dr. Julie Gomez.

"I'm faced with a very difficult case. All his reactions seem very normal; all tests show a man with no symptoms of unreality or sequels of stress. Depression, I do not think he has ever known; neither stress. No scar of any youth drama seems apparent. Of course, he has reflexes that may strike us as odd, but I think they should be attributed to cultural factors. Despite the obsession that the patient feels about our hospital, I think Timi is very, very sane and well balanced, perhaps more than any of us here."

"Come, come, my dear colleague," the head doctor interrupted. "Do not get carried away. You know as much as we do how fuzzy and mobile the line between a healthy being and a pathological case is."

"Yes, I do know. But I think we should look for the origin of the problem with means other than psychoanalysis."

Dr. Martinon, a young, bearded psychoanalyst with tousled hair, spoke from behind his thick glasses:

"You all know I am a follower of Jung's theory. I think we are dealing with a case of cultural misunderstanding. How can we claim to study and heal people issued from a culture that is totally alien to us? We must absolutely undertake extensive studies of the Polynesian myths and legends, which will help us to understand the history and sociology of Polynesia. And we must do this quickly."

149

Alex W. du PREL

"No, my dear colleague, Jungianism proved to be quite marginal. We will not repeat that debate here."

"How dare you claim to understand these people when you do not even speak their language?"

"Come, come, Dr. Martinon. We have interpreters and you know it. And we use the method of Klein, as we do with children who can't speak, where there is a language barrier. Therapy with symbols has been proven over decades, and Professor Kamitzov applied them with great success in Africa."

"But we are not in Africa. We face a society that did find itself isolated for over a millennium, without any external input. Inevitably, such prolonged isolation has created unique values."

The chief doctor began to lose a bit of his calm:

"Dr. Martinon, I beg you not to start the same argument every time we are faced with a patient who does not speak French. We have understood your message in the past, believe us! We respect your point of view. But we continue to believe that you follow a path that leading experts have declared to be a dead end, and that was long ago."

And he turned to Julie:

"Continue, dear colleague!"

"Timi seems to live in total harmony with his personality. It is not aggressive, and most important, he never had any crisis, nor any sign of depression. Early in his stay, I was considering the possibility that his excessive happiness might be an indication of maniac psychosis. But there is no over-activity, no nervousness in his manner, and maniac psychosis only lasts a few months. No, Timi is of a happy nature. He seems to enjoy everything that life presents, seeing it from a good and positive angle. In today's world, which is so complex and insecure, and in our societies, which are so stressful, I feel Timi is like a breath of fresh air; like a breath of simplicity from another time. You want my diagnosis? Well, I declare him to be of great intelligence with untouchable innocence added."

"So we can release him from the hospital?"

"Oh no! Because the minute we force him to leave, we traumatize him. It is as if a superior voice ordered him to stay here."

"So he is not healed," concluded the chief medical officer.

The conference then continued using more scientific language. There is no need here to weary the reader with terms that are not easily comprehensible to the uninitiated. But it should be noted that Dr. Mercado, a specialist in brain injuries, made a presentation explaining a similar case of obsession that had proven to be induced by micro lesions at the base of the reptilian brain.

Thus, late in the afternoon, after much discussion and hesitation, the committee of doctors decided to send Timi to France to undergo micro-radiographs and scanner examinations, despite strong protests from Dr. Martinon, who persisted in seeing solely a cultural factor in Timi's obsession.

As vacation time neared, Julie offered to accompany Timi to France, announcing that she would benefit from presenting this case to the famous Professor Sonnblum. The committee approved unanimously.

Julie then explained the purpose of the voyage to Timi. She mostly had to convince him that this departure was not an eviction from Vaiami, just a temporary absence. But as total mutual trust had been established between them, there was no problem. Timi even seemed pleased to learn that he would fly away in one of the great planes that he had seen at the airport.

IX weeks later, they boarded the Air France Boeing 747 for the never-ending 22-hour flight to Paris. Julie congratulated herself for having offered to be Timi's escort. They spent the first week visiting Paris, certainly one of the most beautiful cities in the world. She loved to witness the joys and surprises of the young man facing an unknown modern world, and his astonishment to discover such crowds, tall buildings, and subways; all this with wonderful freshness and spontaneity. She felt privileged to witness such innocence and increasingly appreciated the companionship of the young man. Julie also realized that changes were happening within her. With surprise, she discovered that she now felt more at ease with her Tahitian patient than with her fellow Frenchmen. The Parisians seemed to run like robots, shut within themselves and impassive to their neighbors. She realized now that a mutation of her basic values had taken place during the years that she had spent in Tahiti. And these new sensibilities were tangible proof of her successful assimilation into the small world of Polynesia. A short visit to the *Maison de Tahiti* on the Avenue de l'Opera, where they were welcomed with great warmth and kindness, seemed to her almost like a homecoming.

But now was the time to submit Timi to the prescribed examinations. The second week was devoted entirely to the interminable waits in the hospitals of the *Assistance Publique*. A consultation of a few minutes demanded days of patience and tons of paperwork, and even being herself a physician, Julie was unable to speed up the bureaucratic monster. She suffered from seeing the efficiency of French medicine, once one of the best in the world, being totally sabotaged by an administrative straitjacket, a relic of another century.

Finally, test results in hand, she made an appointment with Professor Sonnblum, her mentor, the very man who had taught her all his knowledge with much patience and dedication.

The professor was waiting impatiently. The reunion was extremely warm and emotional. The professor expressed his joy to see her so healthy, so radiant, so peppy:

"My dear Julie, you really have not changed. Quite the contrary, you seem very fresh, all sparkling. Being in the colonies seems good for you. What a pleasure to see you so well. Far too many widows dry up and die after the loss of their companion. But with you, it really is not the case. Your choice to go into exile was undeniably a smart move. Come on, tell me! What's going on that's so exciting on the other side of the world?"

"A lot of things, Professor. It's incredible. You would be thrilled. I'm sitting in the front row. I'm a witness to the forced introduction of the kind of society that should ensure a long prosperity for our profession. It is the initiation of Polynesians to the joys of conspicuous consumption. Yet, nobody tells them the price they will have to pay in the future. I witness the senseless repetition in Tahiti of all the stupid errors that have already been made in so many other places. Sometimes this makes me feel very sad, but the kindness of the people always helps me to quickly forget."

"But Julie, since you feel this way, you should probably explain to people that it is dangerous."

"No, no. Unfortunately the people themselves, particularly their leaders, want to adopt that type of system. How can one explain to these innocent people that money has little to do with the wealth and happiness of man? That the type of society that is being put in place is basically rigged to create and perpetuate the privileges of the owning classes. And that to achieve their goal, they use the same ruthless weapons that have proven to so successfully destroy other societies that dared to be different: bureaucracy and its relentless standardization.

153

"I am not some Don Quixote fighting windmills, but sometimes I feel like I am the spectator of the endless funeral of a civilization so unique and subtle that one must invest at least ten years just to begin to understand it. If you'd like, professor, I could talk for hours about what is happening in Tahiti. But, alas, in the social cataclysm I am witnessing, I find undeniable evidence and daily proof of all the theories you taught me. Everything is so much clearer in a small place like Tahiti that is more simple, so much more transparent... but also more cruel."

"Thanks for the kind words, my dear Julie; thank you a thousand times really. But, it seems you have also brought a native specimen of the disease created by modernism!"

"Oh no! The patient with me is a very special case. A great enigma. He fell into our arms one day, apparently coming from nowhere, like a man from outer space."

Julie then explained in great detail the phenomenon that was Timi. For two hours, the professor listened, fascinated. He absorbed every detail, questioned, examined the test results of the micro x-rays and scanner, and studied Julie's notes. Then they called Timi in, and Julie introduced the two men. The teacher was very impressed by the athletic young man who wore his never-changing, beautiful smile.

"What a handsome man, my dear Julie. Now I better understand your dedication. Are they all like that in Tahiti? To see this young man, now I understand the reputation of Tahitian women in the world! Does he speak French?"

"Yes, some. Enough for a conversation," she replied, feeling a blush on her face.

The professor, assisted by Julie, devoted an entire day to doing a series of psychological tests on Timi. Finding no concrete evidence to explain Timi's obsession, he even ventured one afternoon on a path that he only rarely used because it could be dangerous: hypnosis. Even this extreme method couldn't unlock Timi's secret obsession with the hospital. Timi quickly went to sleep, proof of an absence of stress.

"Why do you insist on staying at Vaiami Hospital?" asked the professor.

"Because it's my home," Timi answered out of the depth of his sleep.

"Why is it your home?"

"Because my father told me so, because I know it's my home."

"But Vaiami is a hospital; it belongs to the government. Thus it can't be your property."

"I do not know about such things. But in Vaiami, I'm at home."

Despite a lengthy interrogation along the same lines, the professor failed to find a more plausible explanation. He then explored the emotional personality of Timi, but interrupted the trance when Timi revealed having deep feelings for Julie, who then became embarrassed.

After having slowly woken Timi, the professor spoke face to face with Julie:

"For me, this man has a deep obsession. I can even identify a mania, a state of frank anxiety. You've tried everything. There remains only electric shock treatment. Do you agree?"

"If you think it is necessary, my teacher, I can only follow you. We must heal him. He is a being so kind, so positive, and so little is needed to give him a normal life! But you'll put him under anesthesia, will you?"

"Of course. So come tomorrow morning I'll call the team."

155

THE next day, Timi was lying on a mobile operating table. The anesthesiologist put him to sleep, and then the table was pushed through the door to the amphitheater of the university center. The room was packed as many interns had been summoned to assist with the operation. Electric shock therapy has become very rare these days, having been increasingly replaced by chemotherapy, treatments that use chemical hypnotics, or neuroleptic drugs to induce shock.

The nurses placed electrodes around Timi's head, while the professor explained to the students the unilateral use of electrodes to better target the desired area of the brain. The half hour that followed was one of the most painful moments in Julie's life. She could not bear to see the young man's body react whenever an electric shock passed through his brain. It was a horrible sight. Sometimes a leg, sometimes a relaxed arm suddenly stretched, with spasms, despite the harnesses that held them in place. Timi was no more than a remote controlled puppet. Julie begged them to stop. She collapsed on the bench crying. When the treatment finally ended, she rushed to Timi, snatched the electrodes, and then, sobbing, shook her head against his chest.

Timi awoke half an hour later, little by little, but it took more than an hour for him to entirely regain his senses. He complained of headaches and Julie brought him aspirin. He went back to sleep. Julie sat motionless by his side for long hours, crying constantly.

The professor arrived early in the afternoon. Timi had just woken up again. He had eaten a sandwich was sitting on the bed. Julie's eyes were still red.

"So how is our Polynesian doing? He seems to have tolerated the treatment very well."

"Yes, everything is fine now. But I did not remember such violence with electric shocks," Julie replied.

"Come on, Julie. Our patient did not feel anything. Maybe you have more than professional feelings for this patient. Ah, this bloody maternal instinct! Well, let's see if we got results."

He grabbed a chair, sat facing Timi, and asked the same questions as before. But Timi's answers remained identical; his obsession with the Vaiami Hospital persisted. The professor let out a deep sigh:

"This is a very tough case. Julie, we must try chemotherapy. A new type of Chloropomazine just arrived on the market. It seems that its action on the dissolution of delusions is extraordinary. We could begin treatment the day after tomorrow!"

"But Professor, aren't there dangers of side effects with these neuroleptics?"

"Very minor. Especially baldness. Your Timi could become bald. There is a 50% chance. But better to be bald and sane, is that not so? So I'll be waiting for you the day after tomorrow at eight."

Julie did not answer. She was totally distraught. The professor left.

That evening, Julie and Timi dined at the *Lorraine*, a well-known restaurant on the Place des Ternes. Julie wanted to be forgiven for having inflicted such harsh treatment on Timi. She bought him a blazer, white pants, a nice shirt, and a silk scarf. Timi looked superb, and she was proud to be seen with such an elegant looking man. She ordered a bottle of the best wine, then a second, which finally helped her to forget the terror she had felt in the morning at the university. Timi, very intuitive like all uncomplicated people, felt that Julie was sad. He questioned her, but she remained silent. Thus he did his best to make her laugh, to make her smile. Very happy, they later returned to the hotel. Julie asked Timi to come

157

by her room. She wanted to explain to him that he would now be subjected to chemical treatment, what it was, and that there could be side effects.

In the middle of the explanation, Timi interrupted her:

"I know nothing about these things. I trust you. You decide. And then you bring me back to Vaiami."

Julie then realized how alone she was, bearing the entire responsibility, holding the fate of this man in her hands. She saw again in a flash the horror of the electric shocks, and collapsed into sobs again. She did not want Timi to have to endure the horror of a chemical coma. She sobbed more and more. Distraught, Timi took her into his arms, and hugged her tightly as he tried to console her. She clutched at his chest, and cried. She cried for over an hour. That night, they became lovers.

At four o'clock in the morning, professor Sonnblum was surprised to be waken by a frantic phone call:

"Professor, professor! This is Julie. Sorry to wake you, but it's very, very important. We must immediately cancel the chemical treatments we had decided on. I've been thinking. It may be that we are facing a cultural problem. We must not give him any more electric or chemical shocks. I'll return to Tahiti with him. I do not want to hurt this man."

"Sure, Julie, of course. But there is no need to rush. All the decisions are yours. Maybe you're right. But promise to keep me up to date on the follow up. This case fascinates me too. And you can also call me during the day, you know. The therapy you provide to Timi seems to have taken a new dimension. Perhaps it is better this way! Good night now!" And, laughing, he hung up the phone.

Julie and Timi did not return to Polynesia immediately. They first spent two weeks of exile in a small family hotel in Saint-Jean-de-Luz on the Basque Coast of southern France. It was September now. The resort was deserted. Side by side, they took long walks along empty beaches, silently gazing at the cliffs of Spain on the horizon, and they dined in the few small cafés that were still open.

Julie claimed that this break was necessary for Timi to recover from the effects of the electric shocks. But actually she was the one who needed a break because she had been very much emotionally affected. She needed to regain some balance within herself, to square her ethical conscience with her new relationship with Timi. Their escapade turned out to be a true honeymoon for them both. It took Julie very little time to accept the situation without feeling any more guilt. Quite the contrary, for she had decided that what was beneficial for the patient had to be acceptable, even if it was also beneficial for the doctor.

Back in Papeete, Julie explained to her colleagues the negative results of the Paris tests and scanner readings, as well as the failure of the electric shock therapy. She also announced that she would try a new method to break Timi's obsession. As she had created complete mutual trust between them, and as he had agreed to accompany her to France, she therefore proposed to gradually remove him from the Vaiami Hospital. A few hours at the beginning, then a whole day, then several days, etc. The doctors all agreed. Julie was in heaven. This allowed her complete freedom to continue her secret patient-lover relationship.

Yet, two years of such 'intensive' and very personal treatment did not change much. Timi was willing to leave Vaiami with Julie, even for two straight weeks; but his attachment to the hospital did not abate. His relationship with Julie had now transitioned into a pleasant routine, and the two were living a happy life, although well hidden from all. Meanwhile, Timi made himself more and more useful at the hospital. Besides painting the buildings, he now also assisted the superintendent when detainees were rebelling or developing fits of violence. His gentleness, patience, and cheerful demeanor always had a very soothing effect on excited patients.

THEN one day in December, an old-time resident of the hospital quietly died of old age. The authorities notified his family who lived on the island of Tahaa, north of Raiatea. Three days later, a distinguished Polynesian man with graying hair arrived at Vaiami to arrange for the body of the dead man to be shipped to his island. Upon entering the hospital courtyard, this man saw Timi, who also recognized him on the spot. The two men fell into each other's arms and embraced warmly. The man spoke:

"I'm glad to see you here, Timi. I have often worried about you. I wondered what had happened."

"Everything's fine, *orometua tane* (Mr. deacon)," Timi replied. Then, sweeping with his outstretched arm, he continued "Look how fancy my home is!"

"Yes, you have succeeded. God does help the innocent! May the Lord be praised. Your brother is doing very well, and he found himself a wife. Her name is Mahina. I just baptized their first child, a boy they named Vaiarii in memory of your father."

The superintendent immediately noticed the reunion and conversation between the man and Timi. He ran to inform Julie and the chief doctor. After the man had completed the necessary paperwork for the transportation of the deceased, the chief doctor approached him and gently asked if he could spare a moment.

Meanwhile, the news that someone knew Timi had spread like wildfire throughout the hospital. The entire medical team squeezed into the principal's office to listen to the elderly gentleman.

"Sir, we see that you know Timi!" started the chief doctor.

"Yes, doctor. I've taken care of his family these past thirty years. I am the deacon of Patio, a small village on the north coast of the island of Tahaa."

"Could you then explain how it is possible that nobody in French Polynesia knows Timi? Neither the authorities, any TV spectator, nor any newspaper reader. For three years we have been trying to find where he may have come from."

"I think I can explain. Timi comes from a family that lives in a very isolated valley on the island of Tahaa. When he was still a baby, his father developed a *fefe*, a *mariri*, a filariasis also known as elephantiasis. The disease caused his legs to swell enormously, to the point of appearing to be huge, wrinkled balloons. The father felt so much shame that he dared not leave his valley any more. At that time, Timi's older brother was going to school in Patio. But his father's illness became known to the villagers and—because of stupidity and ignorance—they gradually forced his brother to leave school for fear of contagion.

"Thus Timi never went to school. He never left his valley. His mother died when he was just ten years old. It is the father, the children and I who buried the brave woman on a hill behind their little house.

"The old crippled man and his two sons lived as hermits. They lived off their harvests, livestock, and some hunting. As their valley was considered *taboo* and off limits by the population, I am the only person who visited them. I exchanged a few products against their absolute necessities such as clothes, salt, sugar, and a few tools. I also regularly brought them Notezine pills so that the elephantiasis would not infect the boys. I reserved all my Saturdays for them; the day I spent with them to teach them the Bible so that they could become good Christians.

"Thus, apart from the small religious instruction given in dribs and drabs, Timi is like the ancient Polynesians. He learned to live off the land and forest in total independence and autarchy, totally virgin to any outside influences such as radio or television."

"That's why he has not done any military service?"

"Of course. He has never been registered anywhere. No government official has ever dared to venture into the cursed valley. And then, why disturb a young person who does not know what a war is? He can neither read nor write and knows nothing about the complications of the outside world. Yes, you have before you a Polynesian as they all were one hundred years ago—self-sufficient and proud."

The doctors looked at each other. An angel passed. The chief doctor broke the silence:

"Yes, of course. That explains a lot! But perhaps you could enlighten us on another area. You see, Timi is staying with us because he has a deep mental problem. He has an obsession, a fierce attachment to this hospital here. He sees it as his own and will not leave under any circumstance. We have failed to cure him of this fixation. Would you perhaps have a clue that can guide us toward an explanation?"

After a brief pause of reflection, the deacon started laughing while trying to control himself so that he would not seem rude. But he just couldn't, and now folded in half, kept on giggling. The doctors gathered around him, watching him in silence.

Finally, the old man managed to control his amusement and spoke:

"But because of the *pito*!"

"The *pito*?" wondered the head doctor.

The pastor now gradually recovered his composure. He explained, slowly:

"Yes, the *pito*, the navel! Rather, the *pito fenua*, navel of the land. It is the ancestral custom of the whole, vast Polynesia. Let me explain: When a child is born in the islands, the midwife puts the mother's placenta, umbilical cord, and all cloths soiled during the birth into a bucket that is given to the father. The father will then bury the contents of the bucket on the family land, and plant a tree or set a large stone above these. This act creates the vital link between the child and his ancestral land, a link that is even more important, stronger than blood ties."

The head doctor was visibly annoyed:

"Yes, but this tradition does not explain why a young man from Tahaa feels he is the owner of the psychiatric hospital of Tahiti."

"Actually, yes. Let me continue. I was present at the death of the old man. I witnessed his last words. This is what he explained to his two sons: 'The land belongs to the eldest, because he was born here and his *pito* is buried under the great avocado tree behind the house.' Astonished, Timi then asked the dying father: 'Father, tell me where my land is, since this land is only my brother's!' The father then slowly explained that Timi was born here in Papeete, during his parents' only trip to Tahiti, here in Papeete. His pregnant mother had endured violent seasickness onboard the schooner, and had given birth prematurely upon arrival in Papeete. 'You Timi, you have to go and settle in Papeete, on this great vast land called Vaiami. You see, there is a large house on the land and the people are very nice, clean, and dressed in white.' Thus Timi then obeyed his father and left Tahaa to go to Tahiti."

"I don't understand. How come Timi's *pito* is in Vaiami?" asked the chief doctor.

"You see, doctor, before the opening of the hospital Mamao, Vaiami was the only hospital in Papeete. It also offered the only maternity service in the city.

"Timi was born here, and seeing that the parents were from the outer islands, the midwife probably had the umbilical cord and placenta cremated as a matter of hygiene. The trip to the islands was long and difficult at that time, and to transport rags soaked with blood and placenta in the tropical heat would have created an unbearable stench...

"The day after the childbirth, the father, a man who lived in the traditional world, and who had to give the small Timi his ancestral ties to a plot of land, must have asked the midwife for the newborn's *pito*. To avoid any drama, the midwife then certainly told the father that she had already buried the *pito* here in the central garden. Thus, the father, still reasoning under the old Polynesian laws, now regarded his son as a child of this land, as a claimant on this land, the land of the Vaiami colonial Hospital."

Dumbfounded, the doctors looked at each other. A general sense of guilt kind of floated in the air. Seeing the deep embarrassment that he had created, the deacon quietly slipped away; of course, not without first shaking hands with everyone.

After five minutes of stupefaction, of silence, the chief doctor broke the long silence:

"Yes, ladies and gentlemen, all knowledge in the world is accessible to us. Alas, we ignored a tiny historical detail in history. And we especially lack the basic knowledge of the local customs.

"Dr. Martinon, you were right, of course, and I am the first to admit it. I think it is time to restore the tarnished image of Professor Jung's theories. I would like to ask all of you here to really think about the case that we have just witnessed. There will be a general meeting on Thursday morning. I'll be awaiting your detailed comments. We need to radically rethink some basic data regarding our treatment policy."

The extraordinary general meeting was held with great serenity.

The decisions taken can be summarized as follows:

- Timi is to remain a resident at the Vaiami Hospital. It has been established that he is an extraordinary case because he still carries within him the basic values of a society that has disappeared. He is the equal of a person stepping out of a time capsule. Dr. Julie Gomez has been assigned to establish a precise and detailed inventory of these values, which are to be used as new references for the future treatment of patients issued from rural Polynesia.

- Although Timi does not suffer from perturbations or deviations of character, it has been decided that he cannot function normally in the current environment of modern Tahiti as it has been modified to such an extent that Polynesians living with traditional values are inexorably marginalized and would be victims of intense social drama. Due to Timi's valued services and despite his lack of formal education, he will be hired by the hospital as a paid maintenance laborerworker.

Dr. Martinon, with his usual militancy, strongly insisted that the following observations, inspired by Dr. Eric Fromm and Aldous Huxley, be included in the minutes of the historic meeting:

"Any culture that, in the interest of efficiency, or in the name of some political or religious dogma, seeks to standardize the human individual, commits an outrage against man's biological nature. Conformity is fast becoming a uniformity that is incompatible with mental health. Timi is an example of the freshness of human diversity as opposed to imposed cretinous uniformity.

"The contemporary modern society, despite its material, intellectual, and social progress, tends to erode rapidly in each individual his internal security, happiness, reason, the ability to love. Man pays the failures by more frequent mental illness and despair that hide under a frenzy of work and pretended pleasure. The quality and unshakable foundation of the values of individuals such as Timi are concrete evidence that other civilizations can and must provide an indispensable contribution to the development of a more intelligent society.

"Caught in the vise of uncontrolled population growth and limited resources, humans must gradually evolve from a society of possessions toward a society of knowledge, of wisdom, and especially of cohabitation. Only then will the true wealth of other civilizations such as those of the Pacific islands become fully apparent and necessary. Thus, it must be a duty to preserve the values of these fragile cultures for future generations, as is already being done with endangered plant and animal species. Sacrificing the richness of a fragile civilization so unique to only temporarily appease the gargantuan appetite and vanity of technocrats and bureaucrats would be an unpardonable crime against the future of our humanity."

"The Key"

IN AN isolated valley of the district of Futuna, on the southern side of the island of Raiatea, the father spoke:

"Listen, my son. You are now twenty years old, and you have become a man. Time for you to leave our valley; the time has come to start your own life, to go discover the island of Tahiti. I have endeavored to teach you all the knowledge and experience I have. You have been a good student and I thank you for that.

"Thus you know how to build a nice, strong house; so you should always have a roof.

"Thus you know how to plant, cultivate, and harvest the wealth of the land; so you should never go hungry.

"Now you know the ways and plants that can heal your body; therefore, you should never be sick.

"Now that you have been taught the Bible, you understand the commandments and will respect your fellow men. You are brave and a hard worker.

"Thus you have all you need to prosper as a proud and honest man. You hold within you all you need to be successful.

"My duty is done. I have nothing more to teach you.

"You now hold in your hands the key that will open the door to the world.

"Go, my son. Go and conquer the world!"

The son embraced his mother and his sisters, threw his duffel bag over his shoulder, and went on his way. The father and the sobbing women watched him walk until he finally disappeared behind the hill.

A few months later, sad and skinny, the son returned to his father's home.

"Why did you come back, my son? Did you not succeed?"

"No, Father. The world has become quite strange. I just can't do anything over there."

"Do tell me where I failed, son."

"You did not give me the papers, Father."

"Papers? What papers?"

"Over there, father, you need a paper that says you exist. If you want to build your house out there, you need a paper for the land you want to build on. And then many other papers that say how and if you are allowed to build the house. If you want to work for someone, you need a paper that says that you know how to work. If you want to grow food, you need a paper to plant crops, and another paper to sell what you have harvested.

"They have all kinds of names for these papers: birth

certificates, identity cards, titles, permits, licenses, diplomas, certificates, etc. As I don't have any of these papers, I can't build a house, I can't work, I can't plant, I can't harvest. I just can't do anything. I'm a nobody because I have none of these papers. I do not even exist."

The father lamented:

"My poor son! Forgive me! I didn't give you the right key for life…"

The son answered:

"Oh no, Father, please don't blame yourself. You have given me the right key, the best key any father could have given to his son. But during the past years, the people out there have simply taken on the values and customs of other, far away civilizations.

"They have just changed the lock on us…"

Alex W. du PREL
Opuhi Plantation
Moorea, South Pacific.

About the author :

Born in 1944, Alex W. du Prel is an expatriated American living on the islands of Bora Bora and Moorea, next to Tahiti, since 1975.

After studies in France, Germany, Spain and the USA, he worked as a civil engineer on large construction projects in the Caribbean and South America. At that time, he also built a thirty-six foot yacht that was to become his home for twelve years.

To keep a freedom of travel, the author (a civil engineer) engaged in many, different professions : surveyor, welder, movie actor, mechanic, hotel resort chief engineer, construction superintendent, hotel manager, translator, cook, government consultant, island manager, journalist and editor.

He sailed single-handed across the Pacific Ocean in 1973, then spent a year visiting many isolated islands and atolls of the Central and South Pacific, some uninhabited.

In 1977, he built and operated on the island of Bora-Bora the "Bora-Bora Yacht Club", a small hotel that soon became the meeting place of all long distance sailors of the time. He sold the Yacht Club in 1982 and settled as a farmer, consulting engineer and freelance journalist on the island of Moorea. From 1985 to 1988 he managed Marlon Brando's atoll of Tetiaroa.

Since 1991, he is the founder and editor of *TAHITI-Pacifique Magazine*, the only French language monthly news magazine in the South Pacific.

A truly international man, a specialist on South Pacific affairs and Polynesian societies, the author speaks six languages and writes in three.

Alex W. du PREL is married to a Tahitian lady and has three children.

The cover

Acrylic on canvas paintings by **Philippe Dubois**. This French painter, longtime friend of the author, is living on the island of Moorea (10 miles from the island of Tahiti) since 24 years. He is certainly the most popular painter in Tahiti, an island famous for its artists *(among which Paul Gauguin and Edgar Leeteg),* yet he is still unknown outside of French Polynesia. His paintings, reasonably priced, are available.

If you are interested in his art, feel free to contact the author <alex-in-tahiti@mail.pf > who will forward your message.

Books by the author
Le bleu qui fait mal aux yeux (French, 8 Tahiti print runs).
- *Le Paradis en Folie* (French, 8 Tahiti print runs).
Blaue Traüme (German), Tanner Verlag, Zurich Switzerland, 1992.
Verrücktes Paradies, (German), Tanner Verlag, Zurich Switzerland, 1994.
This book has been a bestseller in Tahiti (a tiny market) and has also been published in German by Tanner Verlag, Zurich, Switzerland, as well as a small private printing run in Japanese.

"G.I.s in Paradise, the Bobcat project", with Tom J. Larson (1995).

English version by the author

DID YOU ENJOY THIS BOOK ?

Want more ?

A second book by the same author
Tahiti Blues
is available

French language éditions of these books ;

Le Bleu qui fait mal aux Yeux
and
Le Paradis en Folie

are also available online.

Thank you for your interest.